Rhino Boy

John Brindley lives with his partner in the southeast of England. He has two children, both of whom have been instrumental in the development of his early stories for young people. John is a keen music fan and enjoys playing squash and socialising in London.

PETERS

FRASER

&

DUNLOP

503/4 THE CHAMBERS
CHELSEA HARBOUR
LONDON SW10 0XF

AGENT: *RC*

ROYALTY SHEET N°- *216910100*

PUBLICATION DATE: *JULY 2000*

CATEGORY: *CHILD F*

Rhino Boy

John Brindley

Dolphin Paperbacks

To my mother

First published in Great Britain in 2000
as a Dolphin paperback
by Orion Children's Books
a division of the Orion Publishing Group Ltd
Orion House
5 Upper St Martin's Lane London WC2H 9EA

A catalogue record for this book is
available from the British Library

Typeset at The Spartan Press Ltd,
Lymington, Hants
Printed in Great Britain by
The Guernsey Press Co. Ltd, Guernsey, C.I.

ISBN 1 85881 797 8

One

Ryan

He looked in the mirror, first thing Monday, guess what?

First thing Monday morning, getting washed in the bathroom, would you believe it? Only a great big spot, wasn't it.

A great, massive, great, furious, red spot right in the middle of his forehead.

You know what it's like. You haul yourself out of bed Monday morning for school – don't you just hate that? Dragging yourself into the bathroom to wash the deep sleep out of your face – your face has this other thing erupting from it. Big. Red. Throbbing. Right where everyone can see it.

Ryan looked at it in the bathroom mirror. 'Oh no,' he sighed. 'I don't believe it.'

Right where everyone can see it.

He'd just had his hair cut short too. Before Friday his fringe would have kept the red eruption hidden. But now! Now look at it! Just look at it!

Ryan's shoulders sagged in the bathroom mirror.

All of a sudden, a thundering at the bathroom door. Danni was squealing away like a squeezed rat outside.

'Ryan!' Dan was going, crashing at the thumped door. 'I've got to go! I've got to go!'

'And I've got to dry myself,' Ryan shouted back, holding the towel to his forehead.

'Come out! Come out! Come out!' Dan was mashing, crashing outside.

Ryan threw open the door, pretending he was still wiping his face with the towel as he came out.

Dan, dashing in like a lunatic, didn't notice anything. She didn't even notice as Ryan aimed a quick swipe on the way past. It missed, mainly because Ryan's heart wasn't in it.

'Don't make a fuss,' he said to his mum, who always, always made a fuss.

'That's a very nasty spot,' she was saying to him, the mother hen, fussing and clucking round him.

'Mum, don't make a fuss.'

'That's a boil, that is,' she started saying. 'That's much worse than a spot. That's a boil.'

'Mum! Leave it, will you?'

Ryan's mother, buttering toast like a woman violently scraping the heads off boils, shook her nagging head. 'Here,' she said, placing Ryan's plate down hard on the table-top.

'I don't want any,' Ryan said, fingering the lump on his head.

'Eat,' his mother said. 'And leave that boil alone.'

'It's not a boil,' Ryan was saying as Danni came into the room.

'What's not?' Dan wanted to know.

'Everything that's not a boil, you div-head,' Ryan said.

'Ryan's got a boil! Ryan's got a boil!' Dan was going, laughing at Ryan's red head.

'I'm going to do you,' Ryan said, making a fist across the table.

'Stop it, both of you!' their mother told them. 'Dan, just you sit down and eat something.

'Where are you going?' she said, as Ryan got up from the table.

'To school, where else would I be going?' he said, collecting his things together.

'But you haven't finished your breakfast.'

'I've had enough.'

'You'll be hungry before lunch.'

'Then I'll buy something to eat.'

'Yes,' she said, Ryan's fussing mother, trying to do up his tie neatly, 'then you'll be buying rubbish. Sweets, I suppose.'

'You're choking me,' he said, shoving his mum's hands away from his throat.

'You'll be living on chocolate and crisps. That's how to get boils, that is,' she said.

'Ryan's got a boil! Ryan's got a boil!' Dan was chanting as Ryan stormed out of the house, steaming, his neck wild and red as the blotch on his forehead.

'**Y**ou wanna watch it,' Ryan said, taking little Anil Patel by the arm, giving it a twist. 'You watch what you say, you hear me?' he said, yanking the lad's arm up behind his back.

'What did he say?' Terry, Ryan's mate, asked.

'He knows what he said,' Ryan said, shoving Anil away.

The truth is, Ryan didn't want to have to tell Terry what Anil had said. Ryan had heard enough about the red blotch on his head, without having to tell Terry about how Anil had said it looked like the red ruby his sister wore on her forehead. The truth is, Ryan was sick of having to put up with all the micky-taking from the others. He wasn't going to let any little, half-formed squint like Anil Patel get one over on him.

'What you doing?' Terry said to him, getting hold of Anil, pulling him back. 'What did he say to you?'

'He knows what he said,' said Ryan, not wanting to repeat it.

'Hey, Jim,' Terry called over to Jimmy Wire. Jimmy, tough as wire, his shaven head billiard-bald, a cigarette held to his lips like a nail. He had been leaning against the wire-mesh fencing. Jimmy Wire, on the fence, boots and no books. Definitely boots, no books.

'Hey Jim. Here, listen.'

Little Anil was looking on with big, open, helpless eyes. Ryan watched him looking at Jimmy Wire as he heaved himself off the fence, as Jim slow-swaggered threateningly to stand in front of Anil. Who watched. Who watched.

'This little toe-rag,' Terry went on, toughing it up in front of tough Jim, 'this piece of toe-jam – he only went and said something about Ryan. What's Ryan done about it?'

'I didn't mean it to be–' Anil started to say.

'Shut it, toe-rag!' Terry went, full of second-hand menace, with Jim wired for a fight right there in front of them.

'What did he say?' Jimmy, coolly, asked.

'It doesn't matter what he said,' said Terry, 'he said something about one of us, that's all. We don't let them get away with it, do we Jim? We just don't let them, do we Jim?'

Ryan was watching what was happening. The spot on his forehead, big, red and nasty as it was, wasn't worth all this – it wasn't worth Jimmy Wire's nail-hard concentration, or Terry's malicious involvement. It certainly wasn't worth that look on Anil's face as he was outnumbered, surrounded, isolated. The spot wasn't as bad as this, as all this *trouble*.

'Smack him one,' Jimmy Wire said, just as if it was any old thing.

Ryan watched Anil's face: his eyes as he blinked; his mouth slightly opening, swallowing.

'Go on,' Jim Wire said to Ryan, 'smack him one.'

Ryan watched as Anil looked up at him. He looked down at Anil's swallowing mouth, glancing, briefly, at Anil's eyes.

'Go on then,' Terry said to Ryan. 'Go on.'

'What you waiting for?' Jim Wire said. 'You scared or something, are you?'

'Yeah,' said Terry. 'You scared, or what?'

Ryan looked again at Anil. Anil, slowly, slightly, shook his head. Anil's eyes said No, please, no.

o o o

Ryan awoke with a start, his heart, his head, his hand pounding. Heart, head, hand, all throbbing together, beating out a unison ache to wake him to the pitch of night.

He started up, blinking wide against the dark. Heart, head, hand pounded. Darkness pressed hard against his eyes, darkness dispelled only perhaps by the throbbing glow of red light emanating from the spot. From the pulsating beacon set dead ahead to light his way into the bathroom, like the lamp on a miner's hard helmet.

Ryan pulled the chord to switch on the bathroom light. The light hurt his eyes for a moment or two but they soon became accustomed. It then revealed the extent to which the spot, surely now a very, very angry boil, had grown.

Ryan gazed in fascination at the thing, the redness of the skin gathering, stretching over the swelling blind head like the summit of a little mountain. That's really what the thing looked like now: a little mountain growing. In the morning, Ryan thought, the thing would have grown so big there'd probably be snow on the top of it. Probably there'd be little trees growing on its foothills, and a lake, like a real beauty spot.

He switched the light back off, only too glad not to be able to see anything. But he could feel it. It throbbed against his skull, pulsing, complaining as his feet pressed against the landing carpet.

There must be something wrong with me, he thought, something really wrong.

His head was buzzing, his whole head, his eyes pulsing and popping with the sheer energy expended in having to construct such a beauty of a spot.

He tried to go back to sleep. He tried and tried to go back to sleep. How could anybody sleep when their own eyelids thumped so loudly against the red-seeing flesh of the eyes? No one could sleep in such torment. If it wasn't his head it was his hand throbbing. His heart leaping. Leaping as it had leapt when he'd hit Anil. Hit Anil so hard it had made his heart leap and hurt his hand.

Every time Ryan tried for sleep, every time the boiling pulse of the boil relented half a degree, the image of Anil crying, hurt, hit hard by Ryan's own hand leapt into his skull. Every time sleep seemed anywhere near, the same image flew out as if projected onto the inner skin of his eyelids. His hand, his own hand lashing out, catching Anil's forehead just above the eye, Anil's stunned, shocked and hurt face, his crying eyes.

Then Terry's laughing.

Then almost worst of all, Jimmy Wire walking safely

away in a satisfied silence, his will done, someone hurt. All right by him.

Ryan lay inside the pulse of his own head trying not to remember what he had done. But he couldn't forget it. He just couldn't, could not forget it and go to sleep. The spot already had so much to answer for.

○ ○ ○

There was indeed snow on the very top of the beautiful spot come morning.

'How many times have I got to wake you this morning?' Ryan's mum was fussing round and round his bedroom as Ryan tried to force open his eyes.

He'd lost so much sleep that night, he couldn't open his eyes properly. Now all he wanted was to collapse back into the arms of sleep as they tugged at his brain. He could hardly move with wanting to collapse. His heart, head, hand had all stopped their pulsating for the moment. For the moment Ryan had even managed to forget about the volcanic eruption in the middle of his forehead.

He lay there, still wrapped in sleep's clinging fibres, hearing, vaguely, but without listening to, his mother's cluck and clatter as she worried about some sense of tidiness amongst Ryan's bedroom chaos.

'Are you going to move yourself this morning or not?' she was gabbing, pecking foul at his floor after the crumbs of his discarded socks, her chicken head jerking back and forth, wings flapping. 'I don't know what's the matter with you lately,' she was flapping.

'I'm tired.'

'Tired? Don't you think I'm tired? Don't you think I've had enough with having to go to work everyday and coming home and having to start again, cleaning and cooking for you and your sister? Not that either of you two care. I learned a long time ago not to expect any gratitude, that's what I learned a long time ago. And I'll tell you something else and all,' she clucked, preening her feathers.

Ryan had stopped listening, a long time ago. About the time his mum had stopped expecting gratitude. He was in and out of sleep still, almost hiding in sleep from the farmyard gabble of his mother's voice. He never got to hear the other thing she was going to tell him. He never heard a thing until it was too late.

Then he was hanging from the ceiling by his finger-nails, the snow-capped eruption on his forehead scream-ing red murder for having suddenly been tweaked.

His mother's tweaking fingers shot away to safety as Ryan shot out of bed. He leapt, shouting, stumbling, tumbling out of his blankets, surprised and shocked by the suddenness and strength of the pain.

'What did you do? What did you do?' he shrieked, his fingers clawed in a cage around the spot, protecting it without wanting it touched again. 'What did you do to me?'

'I only gave it a little squeeze,' his surprised and shocked mother said. 'Only a little squeeze. It's gone all white in the middle. It'll come out now, if you give it a little squeeze.'

'Don't go near it,' Ryan screamed, 'ever again!'

○ ○ ○

'Don't anybody go near it,' he said to the mirror in the bathroom, studying the angry redness of the skin around the thrusting white head.

'You've got two heads,' Dan suddenly said from behind him.

Ryan hadn't noticed his little tomboy sister materialising there, appearing now in the mirror over his shoulder, or on it, like a little smirking parrot.

'You won't have a head at all in a minute,' Ryan said, turning, chasing Dan out and down the stairs.

They burst into the kitchen, flying round the table, kicking chairs. Tea splashed out of their cups, over the tablecloth.

'Now then! Now then!' their mother squawked, her long-suffering, feathery body coming between them. 'Now then! Now then!'

'I'm gonna murder her one of these days,' Ryan threatened.

'Now then! Now then!' his mother said again. Whenever she went into one saying or the other it could stay with her for hours, days. Ryan knew she could spend the rest of this week going 'Now then! Now then!' at him.

'Now then nothing,' he said, deliberately kicking aside another chair. Tea, deliberately, slopped.

'Now then! Now then!'

Dan wagged a finger at Ryan from the safety of their mother's folds.

Ryan slammed the table.

Their mother laid an egg.

Dan wagged.

'Look at this thing!' Ryan said, pointing to the thrust and fever of the boil.

'That's a boil that is,' his mother said.

'Ryan's got a–' Dan started, stopped, as their mother reached out with a winged knock round the side of her head. Dan's look of astonished surprise was lost on Ryan, who was still slamming.

'I know it's a boil, don't I? I know that! It's killing me!'

'They really hurt, boils,' his mother said.

'I know they really hurt, don't I? I know! It's absolutely killing me!'

'It's really big Ryan,' Dan ventured.

'Well I know it's big, don't I?' Ryan raged at her. 'Don't you think I know that?'

'Now then! Now then!'

'Look at it!,' raged Ryan. 'Just look at it! How can I go to school like this?'

o o o

At school, all morning, Ryan swooned, dizzy with pain and concentration. It wasn't his schoolwork he concentrated this fiercely on, but the fierce rage of the boiling boil. His head was boiling, waves of frying fat being drawn up through his face, through his very brain, to augment, to grow the mountainous, beautiful red and white spot behind its round sticking-plaster.

His mother had stuck the plaster over the thing for him. He'd nearly hit the roof with pain as she'd pressed gingerly round the ginger sides, the precipitant sides of drum-tight skin. But stuck over with plaster, the thing didn't look quite so bad, not from face-on anyway. It looked all right in the mirror.

His mother didn't bother telling him how swollen the plaster looked in profile, how heaped it all looked from left or right.

All morning at school Ryan's head bubbled and boiled, tightening his whole face as the skin seemed to be gathered up, lifting his taut face towards the forwards barge of his forehead.

Ryan was concentrating so fiercely, so crushingly, that he heard nothing as his name was called out in the class. Terry had responded to *his* name, and was standing at the front looking at Ryan, waiting, as was the teacher and the rest of the class, for a response. Ryan knew nothing but that which was forcing out the insides of his head. He sat in a daze of pained concentration as Mr Davies called him again and again.

In the end, Al Parry, sitting next to Ryan, nudged him, nodding towards Mr Davies.

'Come on lad,' the teacher said, 'wake up. What's the matter with you? Come on. You've got to go and see Mr Llewellyn, immediately.

'Come on lad. What are you waiting for?'

Ryan blundered up and out of the classroom with Terry. He felt detached, confused by the world outside the wrap-around thump of his own skull.

'What do you reckon it is?' Terry was saying to him on their way down the corridor.

They had been called to see the headmaster, Mr Llewellyn. This was something. You didn't get the call mid-morning for nothing. Something was happening.

But for Ryan, nothing outside seemed real, such was his detachment, such was the forward surge of his all-morning boil-building. He didn't know anything of the world outside his boil-build, knew nothing of how the build happened, only that, from the feel of the thrust, he must be getting very good at it.

Outside Mr Llewellyn's office, things became slightly clearer. Jimmy Wire was already there as if waiting for a bus on a summer's day. Jim Wire reclined across three chairs, his arms spread, tough hands hanging loosely. You could just see what looked like a tattoo on Jim's upper-arm, peeking below the short sleeve of his shirt.

'What's happening, Jim?' Terry said as he and Ryan came along the corridor.

'What's happening, Jim?' Ryan heard him say. Ryan knew straight away what was happening, even through the head-hammering he was taking. Ryan knew that both Terry and Jim knew that Anil Patel, his face puffy and bruised, would be on the other side of the head-master's study door. Ryan knew, they all knew, that they were in trouble. And that the trouble, like the spot, was growing worse, and worse.

That evening, Dan was asking for trouble. They were chasing down the stairs, too fast, too fast. Ryan reached out for Dan's back, shoved it. Not too hard, but she fell, stumbling forward, flying head first, going one heck of a crack against the front door. One heck of a crack Dan's head went. The front door-knocker knocked, because she slammed so hard into the door.

Ryan stood back on the stairs, astonished, shocked by what he had done. Ryan watched, almost horrified, as Dan screamed, collapsing on the floor at his feet.

She was thrashing, feet flailing, hands holding on to whacked head. The front door had been knocked nearly off its fixings. Dan folded on the floor, hands holding more or less the same spot as Ryan's massive lump.

Ryan had felt – as his sister was giving him stick about his head-eruption – all the frustration, the anger and the worry, and the fear, of the boil. The toil and the trouble of the boil. The humiliation of today, when the plaster had come unstuck during the afternoon. Ryan hadn't known, how could he? He sat detached from the outside world, until the world and its worry, until the humiliation of the world, dragged him back like a fool. Like an opened, acne-squeezing fool under the closest scrutiny and disgust of all and sundry.

They all gathered, disgusted, around him to see the custard yellow, then nuclear white, of what appeared to be shoving its way out past the sticking-plaster. Ryan had fumbled with the plaster as they had all gathered, looking, a sundry gathering all gawping and pointing and poking – even the spotty ones. Even the ordinary acne-sufferers gasped at the monster blemish heaped on Ryan's exposed forehead. Even Scratcher Addison, the armpit- and nose-probing mathematics teacher – even he passed comment as the unsticky sticking-plaster fell helplessly from Ryan's finger.

'That's a spot-and-a-half that is, lad. My word–' he said, peering forward, his head grey and lined amongst all the sundry peering heads of Ryan's peers.

'I'll tell you what, lad,' Addison The Scratcher went on, 'just paint it blue and tell everyone you're wearing a policeman's hat.'

Everyone laughed.

They all had a good laugh at something Addison had said. Addison! Scratcher! The worst, the hairiest-nostrilled, most foully-armpitted member of staff in the whole school, in the whole world – and every last sundry, and all the geeks, they laughed when Scratcher made a joke at Ryan's expense.

Terry laughed. Even Tel – he laughed along with the rest. Ryan sat sickly grinning, sick and sourly grinning while under the desk his fists clenched white, wanting to be let out. Wanting to lash out.

Ryan had been left with nothing to cover his forehead, and his shame, for the rest of the afternoon.

Terry came over to him at one time to try to talk about the situation with Anil. But Ryan could see Terry's concentration being broken by the boil. Terry's eyes, everyone's eyes, were drawn to the brute force, the sheer ignorance, of what was supposed to have been flesh. Flesh was supposed to be soft. But Ryan's forehead, its dead, third-eyed, centre felt diamond-hard to his ginger touch. The touch of Ryan's own finger burned ginger and near to tears as Ryan made off home on his own, only too happy to be away from there for the day.

Which is all why, when Danni had started on him, Ryan had reacted. He hadn't thought because he couldn't think any more. Any thought, the very root of any idea of comfort beyond the throb and thrust, would be instantly drawn, thrusting, into the throb of diamond anti-flesh.

Dan had said something as they came down the stairs. She started where the sundry had all left off, giving more stick than Ryan could at this moment take. Which was not much.

He reacted, Ryan, to the anger, the shame, the worry and the pain, by shoving Danni clean off the stairs, her forehead crashing into the white wood panels of the front door.

The door went smash, the doorknocker crash. Danni's head went bash, straight for it, right crack, with the forehead butting the white wood hard. The hard white wood shuddered, Dan fell back thrashing, feet smashing, as Ryan stood on the stairs in shocked dismay at what he had done.

The kitchen door blew, out flew Mother Hen in a cluck of distraught feathers, her head hen-pecking forward at Dan, back at Ryan, forward at Dan.

'What have you done?' she squawked, bristling with indignant anger.

'My head's smacked into the door,' wailed Dan.

'Have you smacked her into the door?' she pecked.

Ryan stood shocked, dismayed, with nothing to say for himself.

'Well?' she pecked again and again, her wings enfolding the curled egg on the floor. 'Well? What have you got to say for yourself? Eh? What have you got to say for yourself?'

But what could Ryan possibly have to say for himself? There was nothing he could possibly say when he himself seemed to be so unincluded in whatever he did. The bright boil on his head seemed to say so much, lighting a way, his way for him. But the way was so dark. Ryan could see nothing but the glow of the hideous spot, could hear nothing but the throbbing hum of its red-gathering, feel nothing but the hurt, the shame and the humiliation of it.

Because indeed the spot did, definitely did have more to it than it seemed to others. As Ryan looked at it in the mirror deep into the night, he could feel, could *see* a purpose gathering under its shiny covering of skin, a dark malevolence sent to haunt him.

He shuddered in front of the mirror in the dark

depths of the night, the haunting purpose still growing, still gathering in the middle, the very dead centre of his head.

'What's an incident when it's at home?' his mother was rattling next morning.

Ryan was sitting with no appetite at the table, watching his sister wading into the toast. Danni had a lump on her forehead, a bad one, but nothing to compare with the massive, pointed alp that Ryan could now see if he looked up and lowered his eyebrows. Not that he could effectively lower his brow without risking eyesight-damaging pain.

However much Ryan regretted Danni's lumpy bruise, he'd have traded places, traded heads with her right now. In fact, if Ryan faced the truth, he'd always been jealous of the way Dan looked, the way she easily won favour everywhere, at school, everywhere. It made you want to throw up. Something about Dan made it so much easier for her to get on with people, to do well at school, at sports. It just wasn't fair. Nothing was fair. Nothing.

Ryan was thinking about his father and what it had been like when he was there living with them, and what it had been like when he went.

'What's an incident when it's at home?' she was going, Mother Hen, worrying and scratching at the ground.

Ryan watched Danni's mouth crammed full of toast and envied that kind of appetite. Ryan couldn't face any food this morning, or for the last few days. He was beginning to lose weight, to look ill. Dan crunched in another huge mouthful as Ryan remembered the cigarette smoke of his father's presence, the boiling rages as hard and hot as the refridgerated beer in cans had been cold. Hot and cold, his father's late presence, but always rock hard.

Yes, Ryan, through the innocent sound of crunching toast and his mother's stupid question, through all of the ordinary sights and sounds of now, yes, Ryan could still remember his father's hot outrage, his cold calling for another chilled beer, his hung curtain of cigarette smoke shifting through the room. Danni was not much more than a baby when he'd finally had to leave.

He had gone and left them, Ryan and Danni's father, when Dan was still sucking dummies and Ryan – when Ryan wanted a father. Really, desperately wanted a father.

He had gone, left them to their mother, running from her as she squawked and pecked at his back.

'What's an incident when it's at home?' she was asking, this flappable, feathery woman who had chased away the hard man with her soft stupidity.

Ryan could not, could not forgive how she had made him shout, made him bang the table, smash glasses in the kitchen and put his boot through the living room door.

'What's an incident when it's at home?' she questioned now, having received the telephone call from school.

Ryan could still remember it all happening. He still remembered crying in the hall, curling up on his bed, knowing, having to know, that his father was going for good.

'What's an incident when it's at home?' she asked, this feathery woman whose life, so incident-filled, had never allowed her the opportunity to understand the meaning of the word.

Ryan resented her not knowing. Especially when she would have to find out this afternoon all about the incident with Anil. Ryan resented the fact that she would have to worry at him, to anger him with the continual peck of his own conscience. Ryan resented having to feel pity for his own mother.

He resented and hated not seeing his father, Steve. Especially as Steve was still around in the town. Ryan resented, hated having to hear about him by reputation only.

Danni was all right, even there. If Dan heard anything at all about Steve Bright, and everybody heard things – hard, manly, sometimes frightening things – nothing seemed to register. Ryan thought that it was due to Dan being just that much younger.

They never discussed it. But Ryan still had to feel it. So why not feel resentful? Why shouldn't he hit out sometimes, just to get one back for a change? Why not?

Because it was so cowardly, that was why not. Ryan knew it. He had only to look at his sister's bruised forehead, at Anil's puffy eye. He had only to remember Anil's face looking up into his as they surrounded him, Terry and Jim Wire and Ryan himself.

'What's this incident they want to see me about?' Ryan

found his mother was saying to him. 'What's been going on?'

'I don't know,' Ryan lied. 'How should I know?'

He was supposed to go to see the headmaster with his mother that afternoon. She was having to take the time off work. She worked in the dry-cleaners, came home every day smelling like a chemical vat. This afternoon she'd be smelling like a chemical vat in the headmaster's office on her own. Ryan wouldn't be there.

'Your appointment's at ten o'clock,' she was saying, on her way out, 'don't be late, will you?'

'No,' Ryan said, shaking his weighted, throbbing head. He wouldn't be late for his appointment at ten with the doctor, but he wouldn't be turning up for school after that. What for? No way. She could see to it on her own, he wouldn't be there to watch her worrying, scratching the ground, turning round and round in circles, her head bobbing, wagging.

'See you later,' she said, 'at school.'

'Yeah,' said Ryan, 'see you later.'

Much later, he was thinking.

'What you got that on for?' Jimmy Wire wanted to know.

Ryan was wearing round his head a sweatband he'd been and purchased from the sports shop in town. He'd been to the doctor's, got his prescriptions, been to the chemist for the antibiotic and the special cream, then to the sports shop for a headband to hide the thing.

The doctor, even he had laughed at the size, the sheer weight of the thing on Ryan's forehead.

'That's a fair carbuncle,' he'd said.

Ryan had nodded unhumorously, but gently. Nodding hurt too much to be able to do with any vigour. Any sudden movement and the fair carbuncle tensed and pulsated, sending out alarm-calls of raw pain, shooting unkind claws in a caged grip round Ryan's face. He nodded gingerly as the doctor laughed to see such fun. Ryan disliked him intensely, intensely.

Ryan took the prescriptions from the man he now intensely disliked, got the medicine and ointment from the chemist, took some, rubbed some in, went to buy a headband. Then he was going home to lie down, hopefully to sleep for a while, while the ointment penetrated and soothed and the antibiotics anti'd every single biotic in his body.

But on his way down the road he suddenly saw Terry and Jim coming up the other way. For a moment he thought he'd be able to avoid them by dodging into a shop doorway. No chance. They'd spotted him before he'd seen them. No escape.

'Oi! Tonto!' Terry shouted at him.

'What you got that on for?' Jim Wire said. But whatever Jim said, it sounded like a threat. He was looking at Ryan in his headband as if he wanted to smack Ryan one for wearing it.

'I've got to,' Ryan said, trying to keep his cool. 'I've some special stuff on the doctor's just given me.'

'What for?' Jim Wire said.

'Yeah, what for?' Terry repeated, adopting Jim's truculent tone, but more comically than threateningly.

'I've got this – it's a carbuncle the doctor reckons – on my forehead. I've got some anti–'

'Let's have a look then,' demanded Jim Wire.

'You gotta see this Jim,' Terry said, 'it's something else, I tell you.'

'Show us then,' Jim demanded. When Jim Wire demanded, with his face thrust forward, three hard lines across his lowered, ape-man forehead, there was no denying Jim's aggression, no denying his hard-wired demands.

Ryan had to suffer the lifting of the headband, revealing to his mates and to the all and sundry street the huge mound of tautened skin, jam-packed with biotics as yet untouched by all the anti.

Terry, the good mate that he was, made out he was just about to puke.

Jim Wire though, he stood his ground, staring back at the yellow and bloodshot cyclops eye in Ryan's forehead.

Ryan watched Jim as Jim stared at Ryan's third eye. Ryan felt as if Jim was about to nut him, smash him forehead to forehead for insulting him in so disgusting a manner.

But Jim said, 'There's something wrong with you.'

Ryan stood there in the street. He knew, as Jim Wire said it, that there was, in fact, something wrong with him. Things like this, growths like these, didn't and couldn't appear for nothing. Not out of nothing. There had to be something bad, something rotten and rotting inside Ryan, to supply such bad juice in such a packed-solid abundance.

'That's why I've been to the doc's,' Ryan said, repositioning the headband, 'to get some antibiotics.'

'Antibiotics?' Jim said. 'Can't you just squeeze it?'

'I can't even touch it,' Ryan said. 'Anyway,' he said, trying to change the subject, 'where are you off to?'

'Nowhere,' Terry said. 'Just not to school. They're going to suspend us.'

Ryan stopped. 'Are they?'

'Course they are,' Terry said. 'That's why my old man's going there this afternoon. I don't care.'

'How long for?' Ryan asked.

'For good I hope,' Jim said.

'Yeah,' said Terry.

The three of them were walking along the High Street pavement, with Jim in the middle, Terry toughing it out walking closest to the shops, and Ryan having to step in and out of the gutter. He was glancing across at the other two as they drew on cigarettes, Jim with his index and middle finger already stained with nicotine, Terry sucking on snout like an idiot trying not to cough or feel sick.

'Anyway,' Ryan said, trying to slow his pace, 'I've got to get going.'

'Where?' said Terry.

'I've got to go home, like. I haven't slept.'

Jimmy Wire was slowing the pace now, turning to hard-face Ryan. 'What are you?' Jim turned and said to Ryan, hard-faced and aggressive.

'How do you mean?' Ryan said, glancing at Terry. Terry had a look of half-amused interest on his face.

'You'd better not be bottling on us,' Jim said.

'I'm not,' Ryan told him, 'I'm just tired.'

'You better not,' Jim said again. 'We're gonna need you. That little nerd's gonna get the Old Bill onto us if we don't do something about it.'

'I know,' Ryan said.

'Then we gotta do something about it,' Jim said, speaking like a threat into Ryan's face, 'haven't we?'

'Yeah,' Ryan said.

'We're gonna get the little nerd,' Terry toughed it up over Jim's shoulder. 'And you better be there.'

'I'll be there,' Ryan told them. 'Course I'll be there. Where else would I be?'

Jim Wire looked at him long and too hard. Terry, his best mate, smirked over Jim Wire's wide shoulder.

Ryan stumbled blind from his bed. The ground came up to collect him. For a few moments he lay there on the carpet wondering, What. What had happened? What was going to happen? What was he doing there? What was that strange sensation in his head?

Thoughts at random were diving in at him like falcons swooping. His mother's chicken-rant full squawked in Ryan's face his shame at what he had done.

'That poor little devil. Three of you – and you had to be the one to hit the poor little devil!'

Ryan squirmed, spiralling off the floor in a dizzying pain and a feathery, flailing confusion of falcons and chickens. Birds of prey and frightened hen-peckers blighted his way into the bathroom.

'My son – my eldest – a bully! A cowardly bully!'

The bathroom door clumped against the side of the bath as Ryan staggered forward, reaching for the pull-chord of the light. The chord evaded his hand in the darkness as his riotous head, full of feathers and horn-hard recollections, turned him around and around.

'Well, now the police will have to sort you out. I can't. The police will have to do it.'

The rim of the toilet bowl caught Ryan's shin as he careered across the room, his hand clasping the air, the light remaining resolutely out. He seemed, through heightened, maddened senses, to be able to hear himself crashing about, to feel himself in pain, stumbling some few centi- and millimetres behind his own shoulders.

'And school! What about school? You'll be expelled! You'll be useless before you've even begun! You'll be just like your father, you will!'

Ryan caught hold of the stability of the sink, anchored himself to it, breathing into its hollow cavern. He turned on the taps to give his ears some sound beyond the rush of his own poisoned blood.

'You'll be just like your father, you will! Useless! Useless! Useless!'

His breath sucked and blew into the swirl of the water. He dipped his hands, throwing cold water against the raw blister of his face. The contrast of cold against the heated rage pounding his head inside out, staggered him. His whole face seemed to hiss and steam like the surface of an iron spat upon. He went to scream.

His mother had screamed: 'You're your father's son! Not mine! Not mine!'

Ryan reeled back, his hissing, steaming face screamless in the passion of his mother's denial of him.

'You're *his* son, not mine!'

His head thrashed. Water, newly heated from his face, dropped onto his chest, ran to soak the waistband of his boxer shorts. The pull-chord from the ceiling light switch dropped into his hand. He pulled. The light came on with the reverberating buzz of the extractor fan.

Ryan's full, furious face came up instantly, framed and

glorious in the bathroom cabinet mirror. He stopped, his stopped mouth dropped in a surprised horror. The fan whirred in his ears like the buzz and reverberation of his own head.

o o o

Ryan's mother, troubled but asleep, heard nothing of the thrash and flail of her son. Her bully-boy nightmares clocked on and off into the night, oblivious to the rant and reverberations in the bathroom. She breathed on in her near-to-no-rest sleep until she felt something there outside the thin, troubled sheets. Her beak clacked open and closed as she heard somebody fumbling in the dark at her bedside table lamp.

She sat up suddenly as the lamplight blinked on to show the figure standing over her. Her night-time eyes focussed slowly on the face floating above her. She took a moment or two to ascertain that this was no longer a dream, but still another nightmare. She looked and saw that it was real and that she was awake.

Ryan's mother screamed into the night.

'**S**tay there,' she told him. 'Stay right where you are. The doctor's on his way. How do you feel?'

How did he feel? Ryan raised his eyebrows and looked up as if to the ceiling. He wasn't looking at the ceiling at all. He was sitting up in bed, looking at the thing, now so painlessly numb, that had sprouted hugely from his forehead.

It was a horn.

No other word could describe it properly. Every other word Ryan tried out on it described it improperly, he was dismayed to discover. Whatever he said to himself, he couldn't deny that he had a horn growing out of his forehead.

The fact that the two-inch-long growth suddenly didn't hurt, at all, didn't help in the least.

'How do you feel?' his mother was asking. How did he feel? How was he supposed to feel, someone like Ryan, with a great, two inch horn rearing out of the middle of his forehead? How was he supposed to feel?

'Oh,' he said to his moulting mother, ruffling her feathers over there by the door, 'oh, I feel just fine, don't I.'

'That's all right then,' she said, leaving his room scattered with her feathers of concern.

The fact that she always managed to miss all sarcasm, all irony in a voice, the fact that she took everything that was said as meant, never failed to annoy Ryan. His mother seemed to see everything so simply, so two-dimensionally. She never, but never understood the pressures, the unseen but powerful forces exerted every which way Ryan turned. She never noticed anything but the horn growing out of his head, always managing to miss the weight and pain of the decisions that had put it there in the first place.

Ryan, left to himself in his room, approached the horn with both of his hands. Now that the force behind it seemed to have abated, Ryan could touch the thing, fascinated and bemused by its numbness, by the neat seam of skin around its base.

He looked at it in a hand mirror. How brown it was, how fading to almost translucent yellow at the tip. He ran a finger up its shiny, rough-grained sides to the perfectly smooth roundness at the summit. He pushed and pulled at it. How hard and fast it was – part of his skull – with a tap-root delving deep into his subconscious brain.

o o o

The laughing doctor came to have a look and a good laugh. Ryan hated him even more than when he had been to the surgery.

The doctor looked and laughed, looked again and touched the horn with an insensitive and intrusive roughness before declaring that he'd never seen anything like it in his life.

Not that this surprised Ryan. He hadn't expected, on visiting the laughing doctor's surgery, to find the waiting room packed with people yawning over old magazines, all with great brute horns sticking out of their heads. People with antlers, it seemed to Ryan, were still pretty rare in this neck of the woods.

Ryan hated the man for laughing. Even Danni, this morning, hadn't laughed. She had looked and looked again. 'Cool,' she'd said. Just that. Cool!

'You should try growing one,' Ryan had told her, 'if you think it's so good.'

Dan had reached out as if to touch it.

'Don't even think about it,' Ryan had told her. 'Not if you want to still be alive this afternoon.'

Danni, with her own forehead still bumped and bruised from where Ryan had flipped her off of the stairs into the door, respectfully withdrew her hand.

'It's still cool though,' Dan said. 'Nobody else has got one.'

'No,' Ryan had to agree, 'nor would they want one if they had. So you'd better not tell anyone, because if you do . . .'

'I won't tell anyone.'

'You promise?'

'I promise,' Dan said, studying the full extent of the growth. 'It's a fantastic colour though, isn't it?'

'Fantastic,' Ryan said.

'Fantastic!' the laughing doctor had said, when he'd arrived soon after Danni had left for school. 'Absolutely fantastic!'

34

Then he'd taken out a little hammer and tapped at it. 'Does that hurt?' he asked Ryan.

Ryan's mum was jerking her head backwards and forwards over by the door.

'It doesn't hurt as such,' Ryan told him, 'but it sends a knocking straight into my skull.'

He laughed, that laughing man – supposed to be there to help but laughing instead, then looking closely, then laughing again.

Ryan hated him. He looked at his mother. She, seeing the frustrated annoyance on his face, said to the doctor, 'What is it, do you think?'

The laughing doctor shook his head. Ryan felt like knocking it off for him.

'I don't know what it is,' he said. 'To be frank, I haven't got a clue. I've never seen anything like it in all my years in general practice. It's quite, quite fantastic! So perfectly formed! In a way, it's really quite beautiful, don't you think?'

Ryan could have murdered him. The doctor was enjoying all this. Actually enjoying it. Ryan could have–

'But what's to be done about it?' Ryan's mum squawked, reacting almost as strongly to the doctor's attitude as Ryan himself.

'Done about it?' the doctor said, as if doing something about it had only just occurred to him. 'Oh, yes. Well, we'll have to get it seen to of course.'

'When?' said Ryan, urgently.

'When? Oh, as soon as possible of course. Tests will need to be done by, you know,' he said, redirecting what he was saying to Ryan's mother, 'by specialists. Oh yes, consultants will be having a look at this young man, for sure. Consultants.'

'But when?' urged Ryan.

His mother blinked, urging the doctor on.

'Well, that's up to the consultants of course. Of course it is. But, next couple of days I would imagine. You'll be getting a call. Two or three days I would imagine.'

Ryan exchanged a glance with his mum. 'What should we be doing in the meantime?' she asked.

The laughing one shrugged. 'Send him back to school of course,' he said, laughing, of course.

Ryan was looking at him. Out of the corner of his eye, Ryan could see his mother. He glanced at her.

She was looking at Ryan as if she could have murdered *him*.

Ryan got a letter.

The police got a statement.

Jim Wire got mad.

Ryan's letter was actually addressed to his mother. She opened it in the morning and read it. Ryan watched her read it, then read it again. He could tell by the look on her face, the way she clicked along the lines of words, that she was having difficulty understanding what the letter was trying to tell her.

Ryan had been to the hospital in London. He had had to spend the night. So many, so many people – doctors in white coats: men and women; consultants in suits: men and women; nurses: mainly women; nutritionists: women; porters: men; floor cleaners: women and men; and men and women visitors: people off the street – had come to peer at him, to take samples of tiny cuttings from the horn, from the skin elsewhere all over his body, from his mouth and his bottom and his ears. It felt like half the women and men in London had been by to look, to discuss, to probe, to lop bits off, to prod and to probe and to make jokes. None of them in the least bit funny. At least Ryan didn't think so. Others did. How they enjoyed their own jokes. Ryan started to question his own idea of what a joke was supposed to be. He'd always thought it was supposed to amuse others. These men and women, all they seemed to want to do was to amuse themselves, at Ryan's expense. Not funny in the least.

Ryan was more than glad to be sent home next day. The only trouble was travelling on the Underground. On the way up there some brat, a little boy with big, questioning eyes, had kept looking at the big bulge in the front of Ryan's woolly hat. Ryan had tried to ignore the stare, but couldn't. In the end, he'd lifted the front of the hat and watched the boy gasp in surprise.

'Seen enough now?' Ryan had said to him.

The boy had sat there opposite, staring, blinking.

Ryan's mother had looked worriedly round.

The boy's mother had a look at Ryan, then turned the boy's face away. But the brat had kept on looking, kept on and on looking.

On being discharged from the hospital, Ryan asked one of the nurses if his head could be bandaged.

'Bandaged?' she said. 'Oh, I don't think that's going to be necessary.'

'Why do you want your head bandaged?' his mother asked.

'For the journey,' he said.

So, in the end, they sat on the tube, with Ryan looking at his bound head reflected in the blackened window opposite.

'That's a nasty lump he's got,' some busy old lady was saying to Ryan's mum.

'Yes,' she said.

'A very nasty lump,' the old girl was going. 'What's he gone and done to himself?'

'Oh, nothing,' Ryan's mum started to say. 'It's a–'

'I fell down,' Ryan quickly interjected. 'Fell down and hit my head on the – on the front door.'

'Must have been a pretty hard fall,' the old lady said, studying the size of the bandaged lump.

Ryan's mother sat saying nothing.

'Fighting on the stairs,' Ryan said. 'I fell off straight into the door.'

The old girl shook her head. 'Boys, eh?' she said to Ryan's mum, who was shifting in her seat, uncomfortable with so many lies.

Ryan was so glad to be home, away from the eyes that would always mould him into a curiosity, a kind of very unfunny joke.

He went upstairs as soon as he could to remove the bandage and look at the place where they'd filed away some little slivers of the growth.

But as soon as the bandage came off, the police came. For a statement they came calling, wanting to know what had happened with Anil that day.

Ryan winced into the bathroom mirror as his mother called him down urgently. He tried to re-apply the bandage, but the mother hen was like a dawn-chorus cacophony up the stairs and after him. She was flustered under the long eyes of the law, with two big policemen sitting waiting expectantly without a cup of tea.

The bandage slipped over his eyes as he came down the

stairs. He had to remove it entirely and brave the stares of two giant coppers in uniform, their questions faltering at the sight of the heavy growth between Ryan's eyes.

Eventually, after much clearing of throats, after many curious glances, they settled into asking all of their questions.

Ryan lied, and lied again.

He lied about the lump and because of the lump. Ryan lied *through* the lump. He followed on behind the lump and the lies, leading the police on with them, telling them lie after lumpy lie. Nothing had happened, he lied. Anil Patel was a liar, he lied. They had seen Anil, he lied, he and Terry and Jim Wire, but nothing had happened. Ryan lied through the lump as the Old Bill couldn't concentrate on anything beyond the lump. They were convinced by it, if not fully, then sufficiently impressed by the lump's sincerity to go away with Ryan's statement unquestioned.

Ryan had told them exactly what Terry had phoned him and told him to say. 'Jim says we've got to deny everything,' Terry had phoned and told Ryan just the other day. 'It's his word against ours,' Terry said Jim Wire had told him. 'There were no witnesses. He doesn't have a leg to stand on.'

So Ryan told the police, with all the conviction and truth evident in the deforming lump, that they were all innocent, that Anil alone was guilty of trying to incriminate them with a mere bruise on *his* face. Against the solid confirmation of Ryan's horn, Anil did not, indeed, have a leg to stand on.

But despite Anil having no legs, Jim Wire wanted to find some way to threaten him still further.

Terry and Jim came round the afternoon after the police had been, to find out what Ryan had actually said to them.

Ryan was looking at Jim Wire, standing in his house like a threat from outside, bristling there, a danger brought in, alien and damaging to Ryan's home safety. Jim noticed him looking, looked back. Ryan looked away.

Terry was laughing and laughing at Ryan's lump. Jim Wire looked insulted by it, disgusted, as if he wanted to knock Ryan's block off for making him have to see it.

'I've been up the hospital in London,' Ryan told them.

'You want to get down the vet's with that,' Terry laughed.

Jim glanced, disgusted.

'Anyway,' Ryan said, trying to change the subject. Ryan was always trying to change the subject. 'Anyway, I told the police we didn't do anything. I said what you said to say,' he said to Jim Wire.

'Oh yeah?' challenged Jim. 'And what was that then?'

'I told them we didn't touch him. I said we saw him, but we didn't–'

'You–' Jim Wire was going, coming at Ryan full-bodied, threatening. 'You– What did I tell you?' he then said, turning to Terry. 'What did I tell you?'

'You were supposed to say we didn't even see him,' Terry said, turning pale as Jim's threatening attention turned on him.

'Oh no,' Ryan said. 'Is that what you told the police?'

Jim Wire turned and kicked the side of an armchair. All kinds of dust flew out.

Terry and Ryan exchanged glances.

'What are you two like?' Jim shouted over the armchair dust. 'What do I have to do? Listen,' he said, raising a huge, hard fist. 'See this,' he said, holding the fist in front of Ryan's face, then Terry's, 'this is going to sort it out.'

He was looking in slow turn at Ryan, then at Terry. 'You hear me, you two useless morons? This is going to sort it out, once and for all.'

○ ○ ○

All that night, Ryan pictured Terry's pale face as he'd swallowed and blinked at Jim's threatening fist. All night long, Ryan blinked and swallowed, blinked and swallowed, hot with worry, his horned head pounding at all the danger and the trouble.

Next morning, his mother appeared like another troubled dream in a fluster of consternation. 'There's a letter,' she told him, even before his hurting eyes could properly focus.

'What? What?'

'A letter. Downstairs.'

'A letter? What?'

'From the hospital. You'd better come down.'

She opened it downstairs. Ryan watched her fumbling with the envelope.

Dan came down and stood yawning and scratching in T-shirt and shorts.

Ryan watched his mother fumble opening the envelope, accidentally tearing the letter inside. He shuffled, impatient to find out.

But he didn't really want to find out. He watched as his mother pecked at the words on the page. He ached with having to want to know what he didn't really want to find out. Nothing about the growth could possibly be good news. As the thing had flowered forth into the air, still growing, so its trouble had thickened and spread, enfolding every last aspect of his life.

He had to watch and wait while his mother's jutting head missed the meaning of the words, as she read and re-read without understanding what it was all getting at.

'What does it say?' Danni yawned, not really caring less either way.

'It says,' their mother said, frowning over the half-torn sheet, 'something about the tests showing . . . showing . . . What did it say now?' she said, frowning, re-reading, re-reading.

Ryan was hopping from one foot to the other. He didn't want to, but had to, had to, had to find out. He squirmed as his mother's chicken-frown delved deep, deeper.

'Where is it now?' she said. 'Where was that bit where it said about–'

Her pecking head came up, surprised to find the torn sheet torn from her hand. She glared at Ryan as he scuttled to the other side of the table, reading as he went.

'What's it say?' Dan said.

'It says,' said Ryan, 'hang on. It says . . . It says the growth is benign, that's what it says.'

'Oh my God!' flapped their mother, her legs buckling under her, nearly falling onto the floor in a fainting fit.

o o o

'Get me a glass of water,' Ryan's mother clacked, buckling into one of the chairs round the breakfast table.

'No, it's all right,' Danni said.

'It's not,' she said. 'Get me some water.'

Ryan was standing there ashen-faced, his forehorn set brown and dark against the white ash of his forehead.

'No,' Dan was saying, handing her mother a cup of cold water, 'it means it's all right. Benign – it means it's not harmful.'

'Not harmful?' ashen-faced Ryan was asking, staring at his little sister.

'Benign,' Danni said. 'It means it's not, you know, going to do any more harm than just being there.'

Ryan and his mother were both staring at Dan. She, embarrassed, shrugged her shoulders, smiled.

'How do you know?' her mother asked her.

'Yeah,' Ryan said, 'you would have to know, wouldn't you?'

'I can't help being a genius,' Danni said, shrugging, smiling, 'can I?'

'No, but you can help being a smart ar–'

'Leave her alone,' their mother interrupted. 'Why must you always have a go at her, just because she's cleverer than you?'

Ryan's hands tightened in anger on the piece of paper he was holding. His attention looked as if it was redirected back onto the page. But he wasn't really reading. He couldn't read in this moment of anger in which his sister, his little stupid sister, was reaffirmed as the clever one of the two. Why did it always have to be so easy for her? Dan had to smile and shrug, embarrassed at being so naturally clever. Why is the world so unfair? Why?

'Is that really what it means, Dan?' her mother asked.

Ryan could feel, he could actually feel Danni's nodding, embarrassed grin.

'Thank God for that,' she said. 'What else does it say, Ryan?'

Ryan concentrated, hard, bringing back the words in front of him to some semblance of order, ordered against his exasperated anger. 'It says,' he said, 'it says that the growth's benign, that it consists, it says, largely of compacted matter not unlike hair.

'Hair?' he said, looking up. 'Hair?'

His mother blinked, shook her head. 'You sure that's what it says?' she said.

Ryan read it again, to himself. He nodded. 'It says hair,' he said.

'Oh, really cool!' Danni said.

Ryan glared at her. 'What's the matter with you?' he said.

'Well, look at it,' Dan said back. 'Look at it. An elephant's tusk's made out of ivory. But you know what has a horn made out of hair?'

'What?' asked Dan's mum.

'A rhino,' Dan said, to Ryan. 'That's what you are – Ryan Noceros!'

All hell broke loose in the kitchen.

Ryan blinked down at the headline on the front page of the *Daily Red Top* that had flapped open on the mat. He had to tilt his horned head in order to read it properly.

"BOY GROWS RHINO HORN!"

'Oh no,' he whispered, picking up the paper. 'Oh, no. No. Please.'

He looked at the close-up photograph of himself, his rhino horn rearing proudly, defined against the darkness of his own front doorway. Ryan read the next few lines with his heart sinking into his socks.

"Your rip-roaring *Red Top* can exclusively report that the boy in our exclusive picture has successfully developed a fully formed RHINOCEROS HORN.
Ryan Bright – Ryan Noceros to his family and friends – has grown a horn from his forehead in exactly the same way as a real rhino does."

Ryan staggered back, sitting down heavily on the stairs. He felt like crying. The newspaper shook in his quivering hands.

How did they know? It had only been a few days since Ryan had received the letter from the hospital. How could they find out?

How did they get the photograph?

The paper shook in Ryan's hands.

○ ○ ○

Danni blinked at the screen.

'Now for a look,' the casually dressed presenter said, 'at this morning's papers.'

Lying back in bed, Dan watched as he held up the big broadsheets to show the different headlines.

"Japanese Economic Decline Affects the West"
"New Labour Euro-Sceptics Bite the Bullet"
"New Beef Scare – Calves May Be Affected"

The silk-smooth, casual announcer read the headlines, making some slight but informative comment after each one. Danni watched his casual red jumper, his heavily jowled face fresh from an early razor.

'Now to the tabloids,' he said, holding up the first of the smaller papers.

"Nips Go Broke!"
"PM Says OK to EU!"
"Mad Cow Mothers Drive Calves Crazy!"

The heavy, smooth face smiled out at her, blandly telling Danni the stories behind the headlines, bringing everything down to the same everyday level of ordinary early morning cosy conversation.

'And lastly,' he told Dan, lastly, 'an unusual story has hit the headlines in this morning's *Daily Red Top*. This,' he said, holding the headline up to the camera, 'is the story of a teenager that, according to the *Red Top*, has grown a rhinoceros horn in his forehead.'

Dan sat bolt-upright in bed.

'The young man's name,' the presenter went on, 'is Ryan, and, according to the paper, all his friends call him Ryan Noceros.

'Ryan's father, Steven Bright, is quoted as saying that the horn has been diagnosed as consisting of compacted hair, exactly like a rhino's horn.

'Ryan the Rhino Boy, is, Ryan's father says, a phenomenon and a wonder of the world.'

∘ ∘ ∘

"Ryan's father," Ryan read, "Steven Bright, is quoted as saying . . ."

Ryan looked up. His father? Quoted as saying?

Ryan looked about the hall, as if by staring, puzzled, at the walls he would find an explanation as to what his old man had to do with it. How did he know anything about any of it? How could he?

Ryan quizzed the walls hard, breathing heavily, heavily. He stared at the photograph of himself framed in the dark doorway.

Someone must have been across the street yesterday with a camera. Someone across the street, waiting for him.

Shivers ran down his spine as he looked at himself, in profile, in the hall mirror.

Someone had been waiting for him yesterday, hidden across the road with a powerful zoom-lens camera, waiting to catch him unawares as he displayed the nightmare horn for everyone to see: in every newsagent; on the buses and trains, in work and in school.

Oh no – school! Everyone would know!

Ryan felt as he had when Jimmy Wire had stood in his home, kicking dust out of his furniture. Ryan felt defiled, his privacy invaded. He had never realised just how private a person he was, how much he valued his own space and time. These things didn't seem like anything until they were invaded, until all your most private fears and embarrassments were brought into so public a display as this horror plastered over the front of the morning paper.

A knock on the door made Ryan jump. The newspaper dropped from his fingers. It was still quite early. His mum and Dan weren't yet out of bed, and here was a knock at the door.

Ryan went over, opened the latch, peeked out. A man stood there, another at his shoulder.

'Excuse me knocking so early,' the man said, 'but do you think we could have a word with–'

'It's him,' the other man went. A camera flash exploded in Ryan's face.

From behind these first two, Ryan heard more voices asking, 'Is it him?' 'Is it him?'

He could hear, see and feel more flashes popping,

seemingly from all over the front garden and out into the street.

'Can we get a few pictures?' the first man was asking, shoving against the door.

Ryan shoved the door back on him. For a few seconds, Ryan thought that the whole gardenful of flashing and popping reporters were surging forward to barge into the house. He shoved the door back harder, closing them out, sliding the bolt hard into position.

The door-knocker started going, and going. Someone was peering with an eye like a camera lens through the letter-box.

The telephone started to bleep. Ryan looked round at it, startled, almost afraid that it was a way in for the hordes gathered on the lawn.

'What's going on Ryan?' his mother was calling down the stairs. Ryan looked to see her standing at the top of the stairs, wrapping her dressing gown round her.

'What's all the commotion?'

'Look at this!' Ryan shouted, picking up the paper, holding it up. 'Look! It's me, on the front page. Look!'

'What?' his confused mother croaked, coming down the stairs. 'What are you talking about?'

'Look!' he shouted at her. 'Look at it! It's me, right on the front page.'

'Oh yes,' said his mum, blinking at the picture. 'So it is. So it is.'

'How did they know?' Ryan demanded. 'How did they find out?'

'Well I don't know,' his mum said, almost smiling at the picture plastered in front of her.

'How can you–' Ryan gasped, having noticed how his mother was almost amused, almost pleased at having her son featured in this way. 'How can you stand there–' he stammered.

'No,' she clicked, changing her mind, 'no, you're right. How could they have found out?'

'Found out what?' came Dan's voice from above them.

Ryan glared up the stairs.

o o o

'I know,' Dan said, looking at the photograph on the front page. 'I've just seen it on the TV. Dead wicked!'

'I'll give you dead wicked in a minute!' Ryan threatened. 'What? On TV? I'm gonna murder you, you little–'

'Now then, now then,' their mother flapped, worrying. She was so far into her phrase-repetition mode, trying as she was to keep Ryan's temper, that all she seemed able to say was, 'Now then, now then,' then, 'Pack that in, pack that in,' and, 'Ryan, Ryan, Ryan.' Her needle-sharp beaked head pointed, dead still, in one direction, then the other.

'Now then,' head move, 'now then.' Stop.

'I don't know what you're so mad about,' Dan declared, 'you're famous!'

'Now then,' she hen-pecked, 'now then.'

Ryan was clenched red and white as a fist. 'What have you been saying to them? That's what I want to know,' he was saying from between fist-clenched teeth.

'That's–' Dan was trying to say, looking at the other photograph.

'Someone's been blabbing,' Ryan was saying to his mother.

'Now then. Ryan. Now then.'

'I know someone has.'

Dan was studying the photographs.

'That Ryan Noceros stuff,' Ryan, clenched red and raw, was saying to Dan, 'that's you that is. I know it is.'

'Now then, now then.'

'I'll give you Ryan Noceros!' Ryan the Noceros was going – going to give Dan something, if only he could get through the now-then cluck and claw of their intervening mother.

'I'll give you Ryan Noceros!'

'Give over! Give over!'

Dan was round the other side of the table with the paper, still trying to read what it said.

'It says here–' Dan said.

'I know what it says!'

'Now then, now then. Ryan.'

'It says that man's your dad.'

They stopped.

They all stopped.

Ryan, knocked back by what Dan had just said, declenched, frowning. His hen-pecker mother clicked her beak closed, her head held slightly on one side as if listening for the sound of worms after rain.

Dan's head stayed down, eyes fixed fast upon the words scattered like seed in front of them. 'It says that man's name is Steven Bright. There's a photo. Steven Bright?'

Dan looked up into her mother's face.

'I've seen him. He's the one's been asking me all about my brother. I just thought he was a–' Danni said, tailing off, eyes drifting back to the smaller photograph under the one of Ryan at the front door.

'What did you think he was, Dan?' their mother asked, soft as feathers.

Dan said nothing.

'Danni?' she said.

'Come on, div-head,' Ryan contributed.

His mother threw a filthy glance in his direction. 'Danni?' she said. 'What did you say to him?'

Dan looked up. 'Steven Bright?'

Her mother nodded.

'He's my – dad? My father?'

Her mother, sadly, nodded.

'He's my dad?'

'Course he's your dad, stupid,' Ryan, kindly, said, 'what did you think he was? What did you say to him?'

Danni was looking at their sadly blinking mother.

Ryan watched them, his frustration, his feeling of alienation – of being left out of their unspeaking communication – growing, hardening angrily inside him like a horn. A hard, alien, alienating horn of compacted hair, shoved, stuck and growing where it doesn't belong.

The telephone started up again. But through its insistent bleeping came no acknowledgment from Ryan's mother or from Dan. They, concentrating, communicating wordlessly, continued to shut Ryan out, to exclude him, leaving him glaring angrily at the never-ending, insistent telephone.

Finally, Ryan stomped to the phone, grabbed up the receiver. 'Get lost you losers!' he bellowed into the handset before thumping the thing back onto its cradle.

'Don't break the phone!' his mother told him, breaking her concentration.

'I'll smash the thing in a minute!' Ryan said.

'You won't you know!' his mother was saying, as Danni burst into sobbing tears, flying by Ryan and running out of the room and up the stairs.

'Now look what you've done!' she said to Ryan, going out after her.

Ryan stood alone, staring astonished into the air.

Look what *he'd* done? What had he done?

What had he done to deserve all this?

What had he done?

The horn, fixed hard into his forehead, insisted that he had done something wrong, that everything was wrong.

How can everything go this far wrong? Everything, *everything* was wrong.

And everything is an awful, awful lot of wrong. An awful lot.

o o o

'Now look what you've done!' Ryan's mum had said to him before going out after Dan.

Look what *I've* done? Ryan was thinking to himself for the rest of the morning.

Look what *I've* done? he thought to himself, peeping out from behind the curtains at the rabble-crowd of camera-carriers and microphone-wafters.

Dan had gone off to school, photographed and questioned all the way. Ryan had watched the press of the press reporters, how Dan's head had to be seen and snapped before the newshounds would believe the whole family wasn't horned, hooved and cloven-footed.

Ryan's mum had also hurried through the snapping, flashing, braying hordes, off to work with her head down and feathers ruffled. A microphone, thrust into her face, had been dashed aside. The reporter had dropped the thing and was left standing voiceless, surprised by the suddenness and ferocity of the attack.

As was Ryan. He had laughed behind the curtain, equally surprised by the sudden rush of pride he felt for his mother.

'Yes!' he had gone, fisting the air behind the curtain. He'd have liked to have gone out there and smashed a few cameras and probing mikes. He would have loved to have shown those parasites what he thought of them. But that would have meant exposing his forehead, naked to the media. That would have meant standing alone, looking stupid on the world stage, with nothing to say but, Look what a freak I am! The wonder of the world, his father, Steve, had called him. Small wonder. Big world.

How often had he watched things on the TV or read about them in the paper without thinking what it must be like for the people concerned. Because, he thought, all the people watching the TV or reading the tabloids were not concerned – curious, amused, titillated, yes – but not concerned. Ryan knew it now. He had learned it the hard way. Ryan had become a victim.

Feeling himself victimised, Ryan had forgotten how he had wondered what it would feel like to be famous. Sometimes, in the past, it had seemed that to be famous, for anything, must be the best thing there is. To be recognised in the street must be brilliant, he had thought. But he had thought that without thinking of the luxury of *not* being recognised and especially not as a freak, a trick, an ignorant entertainment.

Ryan's shame bubbled with anger behind the curtain all morning.

The off-the-hook telephone was stuffed into the cushions of the settee. All the curtains were drawn, the doors all locked. Ryan had removed the batteries from the doorbell. Every so often a rapping would come on the front door or at one of the windows. Ryan tried to ignore it. He sat nervily poised over a cup of cold tea, ignoring the outside world and all its tiny wonder, trying not to think of the hospital visit he was due to make in a couple of days, or the court case with Anil Patel that would be bound to come up sooner or later.

Ryan listened to the voices of the outside world encroaching upon his lost privacy, and felt very, very alone. The more people gathered outside, the more alone Ryan felt. Come lunchtime, the gaggle and rabble were added to by all the gawping geeks from school looking for some excitement.

You sad, sad creeps, Ryan thought to himself, peering through a thin slit of light between the curtains.

'Sad, sad creeps,' he said to himself, looking into the mirror.

The freakshow eruption stood proudly oblivious on his forehead as if stuck there. He studied the join, where the skin finished and the horn began. Marvellous, really. How neat it was, how perfectly finished.

He was standing in the hall, studying himself in the mirror, when another rap hammered on the front door-knocker. Ryan leapt, his proud head turning like a unicorn in the mirror.

'Get lost!' he bellowed at the door.

But the hammering started up again, even more insistently.

Ryan brought his proud unicorn head to the glass in the upper panel of the door. 'Get lost creep!' he shouted.

But then a shorn head appeared as close to the glass as his own, on the other side. 'Oi!' the shaven image shouted back at him.

Ryan could tell whose broken image floated broken but aggressive there in the frosted glass panel.

'Oh no,' he said to himself.

'Oi!' the broken image insisted. 'Let us in.'

'Yeah,' Terry's voice came like an idiot echo immediately behind Jimmy Wire's. 'Yeah,' it echoed, 'let us in.'

'Oh no,' Ryan said, his shoulders slumping, lost unicorn head hanging.

o o o

Ryan let them in. He had to let them in. He had no choice.

For a moment, just for a moment, that fact that he had no choice flitted through his mind. His choices had all seemed to evaporate suddenly. When? He'd given them up to something, at some time, but what? When?

Why?

Without stopping longer than it took to falter, to

vaguely wonder for an instant, Ryan acted again out of having no choice and opened the front door to admit them.

Jimmy Wire stalked in as if he owned the place, with a poor copy, in the form of Ryan's mate Terry, strutting like a caricature behind.

'What have you said to that lot?' Jim asked, turning his threat of a stone-stare straight into Ryan's face.

'What lot?' Ryan stupidly stammered.

Jim Wire looked to one side, as if he was just about to hammer someone.

Ryan shifted with embarrassment.

Terry looked up at the ceiling.

'Is your name Bright, or what?' Jim asked. Or rather demanded. Jimmy Wire never really asked anybody anything. His questions, such as they were, insinuated, insisted that you were *all that* – nothing, in other words. A complete waste of space.

''Cause bright you ain't,' Jim said. Ryan shifted. Tel grinned. 'You're nothing like your old man, are you?' Jim said, insinuated, insisted, insistently staring hard and hard at Ryan's head horn and into his eyes.

'I know your old man,' he said, 'and you're nothing like him.'

Jim Wire was looking intently, too insistently, into Ryan's face, too offensively at the forward thrust of the horn.

'You know my old man?' Ryan said, mostly out of wanting to break the too long silence of Jim's too hard stare.

Jim Wire nodded.

But it was Terry's ventriloquist puppet voice that came, saying, 'He drinks with your old man down the Eagle, don't you Jim?'

Jim, however, was too hard to answer. Too hard was Jim Wire. You didn't do well to get tangled up in Wire, sharp as barbs, just as harmful.

'They let you in the Eagle?' Ryan asked, nervously, respectfully. The Bald Eagle was the pub in which his father, famously, near enough lived, in which his father ruled the roost, drinking and smoking and playing cards and fighting.

'Course they do,' said Terry's unconnected voice.

Ryan broke the wire-hard steadiness of Jim's stare by looking away at Terry. 'They don't let *you* in there though,' he said, 'do they Terry.'

Terry shuffled. 'I never been down there,' he said.

'No,' Jim said, turning on Terry now, 'you never have, nor never will. I don't want you trying to get served in there, making me look like an idiot, like you do.'

Terry shuffled, squirming. 'Don't worry,' he said, 'I don't want to go near the place. Don't worry, I got plenty of places to go, I don't need to try and get down there. Don't worry,' he said, for the third time, as worried as his pale, sick face now plainly illustrated.

Ryan, as he watched Terry squirm, tried to remember why he had thought they were such good friends. Now, with Jim confronting them both in turn – each was competitively trying not to be the one confronted – Ryan couldn't think of anything. For the few last moments of Terry's sick, pale squirm, Ryan tried, but failed, to remember anything on which he could re-establish their friendship.

'Why haven't you offered us a cup of tea or anything?' Jim asked Ryan, still out-staring Terry, screwing him into the ground.

'Tea?' Ryan went. 'You want a cup of tea?'

'Two sugars,' Jim said, turning away from Terry at last. Terry sagged with relief. Jim fell into one of the arm-chairs, his legs out straight as if he owned Ryan's house and everything in it.

'Tel?' Ryan said, feeling invaded by the force of arrogance that was Jim Wire. He couldn't bear to look at Jim's jeans and big boots, with their heels dug into his mum's nearly-new carpet.

'What?' Terry said.

'Tea?' Ryan asked him, looking at him.

Terry looked at him back. For a moment, for a broken moment, they shared a passing look of mutual under-standing, both invaded, but both powerless under the arrogance of this domination.

o o o

Ryan disappeared upstairs for a few minutes to be on his own. He pretended to be looking for something, opening drawers in his room. Perhaps he *was* looking for some-thing? Perhaps he'd find something in one of the drawers, something of his own that couldn't be damaged, spoiled, defiled by anyone.

Under a jumper – some money he'd been saving for a new leather jacket. He blinked down at the money.

A leather jacket? Why did he want one? Why did Terry want one?

Jim Wire wore leather. Everyone said he looked cool in it. Everyone said Jim Wire looked dead hard.

Terry wanted one.

Ryan was saving for one.

He slammed the drawer closed.

∘ ∘ ∘

'So,' Ryan, from the kitchen, heard Jim Wire's voice calling him, 'so you're the Rhinoceros now, are you?' Jim was shouting.

Ryan winced, touched the hair horn on his forehead. So far, miraculously, neither Jim nor Terry had mentioned it. Ryan wondered what on earth he was to be put through now. He tried to ignore what was being said, or shouted at him.

He went to the cupboard, took out three mugs, threw a tea-bag in each.

'What's the matter, Rhino?' Jim Wire's over-truculent voice came at him from the kitchen doorway.

Ryan looked round him at Terry's moon face floating, gloating beyond Jim Wire's wiry right shoulder. 'What did you say, Jim?' Ryan said.

'What, you deaf and all now, or something?' Jim said.

'No– I, no. I didn't hear. Were you talking to me?'

'Well who else would I have been shouting out to about some freak rhino horn?' Jim looked around the kitchen. 'What, are there loads of you out here, or something? Have you started a Rhino Club with all your freak mates, have you?'

Terry was, of course, laughing his own freak head off in the hallway behind his dangerous hero. Of course he was. Your mates, all of them, no matter how close, only ever seemed to be enjoying themselves if you were being intimidated by something or someone. It seemed as if there was a rule that all the lads had to abide by. Or lots of rules. Masses of them, everywhere.

Ryan hadn't noticed before. He'd never stopped to look or bother thinking about it. Until now.

Now, he stopped. He thought about it. The horn, the rhino tusk had set him apart, placed him conspicuously outside the mass of complex rules they all had to live and laugh by. Ryan had become the transgressor, an outlaw, a laughing-stock.

And the subject of Jim Wire's aggressive attention.

'You and your rhino mates must be going about in herds, I suppose,' Jim said.

Terry laughed. Of course. On cue, Terry's laughter. Jim Wire made the rules, established them as he went along. Terry obeyed them, all of them, slavishly.

Ryan, pouring boiling water from a trembling kettle, was the butt, the very exception that made the very hostile rule.

'Sugar?' Ryan said, trying to sound still cool, still uninhibited, still, somehow, dignified.

'Didn't I just tell you, Rhino?' Jim said, with a glance at Terry. 'Did I or did I not tell you two sugars?'

'I'm sorry,' Ryan tried to say, 'I didn't–'

'Did I,' Jim said to Terry, 'or did I not tell the rhino I wanted two sugars, or am *I* the stupid one?'

'You told him, Jim,' Terry instantly said, 'and so did I. Two sugars, Rhino. And make it strong.'

'Are *we* the stupid ones,' Jim said, turning back to Ryan, 'or what?'

He was staring, staring with the ever present threat of violence, into Ryan's face. Ryan was trying to look back at him, trying not to seem to challenge him while not having to back too far down.

'Eh?' Jim stared at Ryan, looking hard, peering down his nose with his head just held to one side. 'Are *we* the stupid ones, Rhino, or are *you*? Eh?'

'Must be me then,' Ryan had to say, backing too far down, far too far down.

He could just make out the pale moon of Terry's face over Jim Wire's shoulder, Terry watching Ryan's face fading behind the hard forehead horn, Ryan swallowing his pride, what was left of it, and the last vestiges of his dignity.

But Jim was still hard-wired into Ryan's faint face.

Ryan had to blink and look away. He sugared all the teas, having been sure to make them good and strong. Ryan didn't like his tea this strong. Neither, he knew, did Terry. But Jim did. Jimmy Wire did so they all did. It was the way.

Ryan stirred all three mugs, picked one up and handed it to Jimmy. 'Two sugars, nice and strong,' he said.

Jim took it from him, looked into the surface of it. Ryan tensed as Jim inspected it.

'You're nothing like your old man,' Jim said, looking up as if he'd just read that fact in the surface of his tea.

'His old man hasn't got a dirty great tusk growing out of his head for a start,' Terry said, taking his tea from the side.

'Tell me this, Rhino Boy,' Jimmy said, loafing back into the armchair, 'do you even know anything about your old man?'

'What do you mean?' Ryan asked, perched on one end of the settee, while Terry stood peeking through the curtains at the army of press encamped outside, in the garden and on the street.

'I mean, you don't see him, do you.'

'Yeah, I see him. Sometimes.'

'Yeah? When?'

'I don't believe some of the cameras out there,' Terry said, without looking round.

'I mean, when do you see him?'

'Well, you know, sometimes.'

'The telly as well,' Terry said.

Jim glanced round, a look of quick disdain on his face. 'No,' he said, 'I don't know. But I know what I think. Do you want to know what I think, Rhino Boy?'

The Rhino Boy nodded. He didn't want to know what Jimmy Wire thought about anything, but the horn on the head had to set him nodding, having deprived him of every other choice he may, in his whole life, have once had.

'TV cameras,' Terry said. 'Sky News and everything, I tell you.'

Jim Wire disdainfully glanced in Terry's direction. 'As you seem so interested,' Jim said to Ryan, 'then I'll tell you. I think you don't know him at all. I think you don't ever see him, do you? Eh? You don't ever see him.'

Ryan was looking down at his mother's nearly-new carpet. Jimmy's big boots were dug in by the heels.

No, Ryan didn't ever get to see his father. No, Ryan didn't know him any more than Dan knew him. But he was Ryan's father. He was *Ryan's* father. That, Ryan did know. And Ryan did know, as did most people, of his father's reputation. That gave Ryan some claim over that reputation. Surely it gave Ryan that. He was entitled to something, wasn't he?

But now, here and now, looking down at Jimmy's red-brown boots crushing the carpet, he felt his claim denied by what Jim was, by Jim's own relationship with Ryan's unknown father.

Someone like Jimmy Wire – people like him – how they could overcome your whole life. How they could so easily have something over everything you had and were. How they did it, Ryan didn't know. He couldn't tell. He only knew that *he* had nothing like it.

He had only his horn, his rhino-headed face to lose. Because Ryan Bright, Ryan Noceros lost face and lost face, until even the way his lost face looked was no longer his own.

'Eh?' Jimmy said, determined to get a response.

'Sky News and everything,' Terry interjected from over by the slit-apart curtains.

'You don't know him, do you Rhino?'

Ryan shook his horned head. He shook his head. No, he did not know his own father, even as much as Jim Wire did.

But Jim would have, would have words of confirmation out of Ryan. Jim Wire wanted the words, not to deny Ryan's relationship with his infamous father, but to embellish his own.

'What did you say, Rhino Boy?'

'I said no, Jim. You're right. I don't know him.'

Wire grinned, cruelly barbed.

'You're really famous, you are Ryan,' Terry said, still peering through the curtains.

'No,' Jim said, quietly. 'I know you don't. But I do. And he's given me a message to give to you.'

'Has he?'

'Yeah.'

'Dead famous you,' Terry was going. 'They're all out there, all of them. Dead famous.'

Jim was saying nothing. He had a message for Ryan from his father, but said nothing.

'What did he say?' Ryan said.

Jim Wire grinned. He had it all, was reluctant to hand over any of it. What Jim had was power, and was powerful in every way.

'He said,' Jim said, eventually, 'that you're to expect him tomorrow.'

'What, he's coming here?'

'That's what he said, Rhino Boy. He's coming here, and you're to let him in.'

'What time?'

'I don't know, do I. He just told me to tell you to expect him.'

'Right,' Ryan said, with Jim staring into his face. 'Thanks Jim.'

'You're nothing like him, you know,' Jim said.

'You're dead famous, you are,' Terry was saying again, his face in the drapes.

'You're not anything like–' Jim was saying.

'Dead famous you are, Rhino,' Terry said.

Jim Wire, interrupted once too often, jerked his head round in Terry's direction. 'Oi!' he spat. 'Oi! Stupid! Get away from there, can't you? Come over here you idiot. Sit down!'

Terry silently sat. Sorry.

'Sorry,' he said.

'Shut up!' shouted Jim. 'You two are really getting on my nerves, do you know that? Do you?'

Terry and Ryan sat with their boot heels dug into the nearly-new carpet, their heads down.

'I don't know what I'm doing here with you two losers, really I don't. And you,' he said to Ryan, 'whatever you say to that lot out there, I'm nothing to do with it, right?'

'I'm saying nothing to any of them,' Ryan said, 'don't worry about that.'

'Well, I *am* worried about that,' said Jim. 'I've got other things going, bigger things, and I don't want you or lap-dog here messing them up, you hear?'

Lap-dog Terry hung his head down still further, wanting badly now to be taken out on a lead and given a run by his master.

'You hear me?' his master's voice came.

Terry nodded like a dog.

'I am worried about this whole thing,' Jim went on, satisfied with the lap-dog's subservience. 'I'm worried about being involved with you two in this kid's stuff, especially with the Rhino Boy there drawing attention to himself.'

'I'm hardly doing that, Jim,' Ryan tried to say.

'Well, you're hardly inconspicuous, are you,' Jim told him. 'Just don't give me any more reason to worry, either of you.'

'But what are we going to do about Anil Patel, Jim?' Terry asked, trying to lick his master's hand.

'I'll tell you what we're going to do,' he said, leaning forwards in his chair.

Terry and Ryan automatically leaned with him.

'I'll tell you just what we're going to do about that little nerd,' Jim said, with an angry vein pulsing in his neck.

Lights on.

The bathroom bulb nearly blinded him as he staggered in, dragging on the pull-chord. The extractor fan buzzed too closely to his ears, sounding too closely like the buzz brought back on in Ryan's brain by lack of sleep.

Then, unkindly-sighted, the horned image reared before him in the mirror. He charged at his own reflection, thudding rhino and rough into the glass. The glass on the cabinet door cracked, quite neatly, in two. A shocking blue light seemed to dance before Ryan's sight, through which two horned devils thrashed crimson in the two cruel halves of the broken mirror.

He staggered from the bathroom in the dead of night, surrounded by threats, confronted by sequences of events he couldn't bear to think about.

But he had to think about them. He couldn't but think about Jimmy Wire, fisted and threatening to frighten Anil Patel into submission. Ryan and Tel had watched Jim's fists in front of them, threatening them as much as anybody.

'We're going to get him to tell his parents it was all a lie. He's gonna tell the police we weren't there. And if he doesn't,' Jim had said, showing his malicious fist to Ryan and Terry. 'Heaven help him if he doesn't,' he'd said.

Ryan shuddered, threatened and afraid of the part he was going to have to play in all of this.

Then there was the visit by his father the next day. Then there was the hospital. Then the press waiting outside another threat gathering, gathering.

Ryan's head buzzed and popped. He turned on the TV, wanting sound, wanting vision, wanting the thoughts in his head overcome by something not brought about by his own weakness and shame.

The screen lit his face as an unhorned head looked back from the box and said, 'What about that boy with the rhino horn growing out of his head then, eh? What's that all about then?'

You tell me, Ryan thought, his sunken heart falling further towards his unbooted heels.

You tell me what it's all about, he thought, please. Somebody tell me.

'Can you believe it?' the late-night comedian was saying. 'A rhinoceros boy? They'll be asking us to believe in the Elephant Man next I suppose. Then the Birdman of Alcatraz – he grew a beak, did he, or what? People are turning into animals everywhere. They are. Tell you what, get a whiff of that armpit next to you on the train in the rush hour. I ask you, is that human? Dear me. No, listen rhinoceros boy, you are not alone. Everyone's an animal, in one way or the other. My girlfriend, for example–'

Everyone's an animal in one way or another, Ryan heard the man say. He stopped listening to the TV ramblings, the disconnected inventions that were supposed to be funny by being true.

Well, if they were true, they were not funny. If a boy grew a rhino horn then he would have to know the unfunny truth of it, the fact of the thing. He would have to know something others would not, could not. He would have to know, as Ryan knew, that it was the truth, and it was certainly not funny.

'So, how you doing, son?' Steve Bright was standing there asking him.

How you doing, son, he was asking Ryan as Ryan stood there in front of him with the pointed bit of a rhinoceros sticking out of his head.

Ryan's head was popping, fizzing with having sat up half the night watching unfunny comedians and an ancient American comedy film where nothing, but nothing funny happened. Ryan thought it was a lot like his life. Supposed by everyone to be funny, what was happening to him, but really there wasn't even a half-decent laugh in it. Not for Ryan anyway. He watched them all, all the consultants and the nursing staff, the on-lookers audienced and amused, looking in through the windows, through their cameras, probing with their microphones and laughing.

Not funny.

Now he was confronted with this man he barely knew, big Steve Bright, his boot-soles pressing hard into the carpet.

Steve Bright had laughed outright at his son's extended features. He had laughed at the press-gang, wet and cold in their cars and vans.

'It's true then,' he had said, as soon as he'd got over his

laughing fit. 'You've really turned into a rhino, eh? Here, show us. Turn to the side a bit. Come on, what's the matter with you?'

All this, and Ryan had not yet said a word. He had nothing *to* say. He stood in awe of the man, his own father, a scarred stranger come in out of the wet and cold, with Love and Hate tattooed onto his fingers. Ryan stood speechless, helpless and confused, as his father turned him round both in mind and body.

Steve Bright laughed out loud.

Ryan Bright reddened under his hero's gaze, wanting this closeness, needing it, but feeling severely embarrassed by the laughter and the over-close scrutiny. Ryan wanted and didn't want, felt glad and regretful, happy, embarrassed, sad, stupid and afraid, all at the same time. He said nothing.

'That's some horn, that is,' his father told him.

'Feel it then,' Ryan went and said, for want of anything else to say. He had to endure those big Love-Hate, near-fisted fingers to touch, to feel, to push and pull at his head growth. Ryan could feel his shame, his ridiculousness growing.

'Hard as a hoof,' his father said. 'Hard as old boots. I've never seen anything like it in my life. Fantastic. What do you reckon?'

'Oh,' Ryan said, stumbling, unable to collect his own reckonings together into any sense. He wanted to impress. That was all. At this moment, he felt he would do anything.

'You know,' he said, 'it gets in the way when you're trying to sleep at night.'

'Yeah,' his father said, wandering off, glancing round the room, quickly, from one place to the next. 'I'll bet it does. Your mum's not here, is she?'

'No, she's at work.'

'Yeah, thought so. Thought it best she didn't – you know – better she doesn't know I've been here to have a few words with my son. You know what she's like.'

'Yeah,' Ryan said, although, in this respect, he didn't. He didn't know at all what it was about his mother that made this man so afraid to be seen by her. She was just a mother hen, while he – look at him – the tough lines of his thin face, the Love-Hate relationship of his knuckles. What could there possibly be between the two of them to make him so– so nervous, so shifty?

'Aren't you gonna make us a cup of tea then?' Steve Bright asked his son.

Ryan was watching him as he peered at the photographs in their cardboard frames on the wall. Ryan was looking at the rolled newspaper in his back pocket, the studs in his jeans belt, the sawn-off sleeves of his T-shirt. Ryan was wondering how his father didn't feel the cold with arms as bare as that.

Steve Bright looked over at him, too suddenly, too aggressively. 'What's up with you?' he said.

o o o

Ryan busied himself in the kitchen, trying not to think

too much, trying not to feel intruded upon by this man, this almost complete stranger. Whenever Ryan tried to think about anything these days, it was never without a degree of confusion, frustration and discomfort. He brewed the tea, trying not to wonder why his father had chosen to come and see him now. Now, of all times. Why now?

He shook his horned head free of all questions time and again. But they would keep crowding back in on him, crowding back in on him like the situations outside, like his so-called friends, like the gutter press sitting wet in the gutter outside.

On his return, two mugs of hot tea in his hands, he found Steve Bright in the sideboard cabinets, one of Ryan's mother's little trinket caskets in his hands. As Ryan appeared with the tea, Steve snapped shut the casket, set it hurriedly back in position in the cabinet. Ryan watched him casually swing the cabinet door shut, amble over, take one of the mugs from his son's hand.

'This one mine?' he said.

'Either,' said Ryan. 'They're both the same. Nice and strong.'

Steve Bright sauntered with his tea over to the dining-table, put down the mug onto its surface. Ryan swallowed hard, knowing that the hot mug would damage the wood, that his mum would get brain damage. But Ryan couldn't say anything, how could he? He himself went over, placing his own mug on yesterday's newspaper, and sat down.

As if inspired by the sight of the paper, Steve Bright

removed the *Red Top* tabloid from his back pocket, slapping it hard onto the table-top.

'They're after you all right,' he said, sitting himself down. 'That lot out there? They want you, boy, know what I mean? Eh? You're in all the papers. You're the man of the moment you are. Yesterday, today–'

'Today?'

'Yeah, today. Haven't you seen this?'

'No, I– Mum must have taken today's with her.'

'Then have a look at that, my son,' he said, his little wet moustache twitching. 'Man of the moment, or what?'

What?

Ryan looked with dismay as his father unrolled the *Red Top* in front of him on the table. 'Oh no,' he said, as the headline blared out at him.

◦ ◦ ◦

Ryan blinked at the blaring headline.

'Rhino Boy Ryan Is School Bully!'

Oh no.

Oh no. Always. Always the bullies and the bullied, always the victimisers and victims.

"Ryan Noceros, the boy that has grown a complete horn, from hair, on his forehead, has been suspended from his school, Priory Comprehensive, for an incident in which a younger boy was allegedly struck in the face. Your rip-roaring *Red Top* can exclusively reveal . . ."

Etcetera.

Ryan nodded at the etceteras running juicy with gossip down the page, flowing onto the next, dripping into the comments column.

The Priory Comprehensive School. They even actually named it. Why would they want to do that? What difference did it make which school? But there it was, splattered with Ryan's new name across the national, sensation-seeking journal.

Always victimisers, always victims.

But look through the newspaper pages, turn on the TV at nine o'clock for the news. Someone somewhere's been robbed. Someone's been mugged, beaten up. Someone's been killed.

Hundreds of people might have lost their jobs through no fault of their own. So many young people are living homeless on the street. So many suffering from fatal diseases. So many hearts breaking.

Always victimisers, always victims.

Ryan peered at the badly reproduced colour photograph of the Rhino Boy. The school bully. He studied the way the photograph showed a sort of cruel, animal leer on his face. He read the account of the incident where a younger boy was allegedly struck in the face.

Ryan blinked again at the troubled, animal look in the frightened rhino's features.

Always victimisers.

Always victims.

◦ ◦ ◦

'Oh no?' Steve Bright was going, jumping up. 'Oh yes. Yes my son,' he was going, pacing excitedly around the room. 'Yes! Yes! This is worth something, this is.'

Ryan was blinking back his tears, the headline swimming on the table in front of him.

"Rhino Boy Ryan Is School Bully!"

And this was worth something? This, and another poor photograph of him sneering like a cornered animal. This was worth something?

Steve Bright was stalking viciously round the room, clicking his fingers. 'This, my son, is worth a few bob, I tell you. More than few bob.'

'How?' Ryan asked.

'How? Look at that lot out there,' he said, flinging back the curtains.

The newshounds sprang to attention like hunting dogs, wet noses twitching in their pointy faces.

'Just have a look at that little lot, my son. Oh yes,' he said, clapping his hands together. 'We are on to a winner here, no doubt about it. Get yourself ready my son, we are on our way.'

Ryan sank at the table, his head down, eyes involuntarily reading the super-sensational report on him bullying the younger boy, the smaller, weaker boy, who was allegedly struck in the face.

'You are man of the moment, that you are,' his father, this stranger in boots and belt, jeans and sawn-off sleeves, said to him. 'You've done good my son, really you have.'

Ryan's father kept calling him his son. 'My son,' he said, time and again. But Ryan, this man's son, could sense, could feel the emptiness of a phrase which called everyone son, making this man father of no one.

'Why, what have I done?' he said.

'What have you done?' the man said back, bounding over to him. 'What have you done?'

Ryan felt himself gripped by the shoulders. He could feel Steve Bright's moist moustache quivering by his ear.

'What haven't you done my son, what haven't you done. I'm right proud of you, I am. Look at you,' he said, nodding towards the unwound newspaper, 'you are a commodity, that's what you are, know what I mean? Know what I mean, my son?'

Ryan, reluctantly, nodded. He knew what Steve Bright meant, even when Steve said he was proud of him.

'Brought yourself into prominence, you have. Brought yourself into prominence. Nice touch, that bullying stuff, just the job. What do you say my son?'

'Yeah,' said Ryan, softly.

'And,' Steve said, his prickly upper lip lapping at Ryan's outer ear, 'a little bird tells me you've got it all sorted as well. Well sorted, a little bird tells me.'

'Yeah,' said Ryan, 'well sorted.'

o o o

'Well sorted,' he said, remembering the little bird on a wire, a Jimmy Wire making a fist, slamming it down onto Ryan's mother's innocent coffee-table. Ryan remembered blinking hard as the fist crashed into the table-top. 'Saturday,' the little bird had said, as Ryan remembered it, 'on his way back with his sister from that church or synagogue or whatever–'

'Mosque,' Ryan remembered Terry saying. He remembered Terry's crumbling face as Jim stared straight into it, dismantling it.

'On Saturday,' Jim had gone on, 'on his way back from wherever he goes, we see him and his sister,' Jim had said, holding up his fist, 'and we make sure they see us, right? Right?'

Ryan remembered nodding. 'Right,' he remembered saying.

'And you better be there, Rhino Boy,' Jim, Ryan remembered, said to him, Jim's nail-hard fist between them. 'You better be there, you hear me?'

∘ ∘ ∘

'Yeah,' Ryan said, the nicotine-scented moustache still flickering at his ear, 'well sorted.'

'That's all right then,' Steve whispered in his ear. 'That's all right then, my son, isn't it?'

Ryan nodded.

There was a tapping at the window. At least six or seven faces were there, peering through the nets into the animal pen.

Ryan and his father looked round.

Steve Bright grinned. 'Your audience awaits, my son.'

'How do you mean?' Ryan asked him, his face draining of colour.

81

'We're gonna make some money,' Steve said, waving at the gallery of faces over there.

'And speaking of money,' he said, 'I need some expenses, know what I mean?'

Ryan, pale and silent, shook his head.

'I need some cash, my son. Just a few bob, you know, few drinks, grease a few palms.'

Ryan sat there palely dumb. A flash light went off outside, lighting up the room.

Steve glanced round. 'The natives are getting a bit restless. Come on,' he said, 'come on. Where's she keep the cash these days?'

Ryan looked confused.

Steve Bright shook his head. 'What is the matter with you? Stupid or something, are you? Listen, monkey, where does your mother keep her money nowadays? In here?' he said, opening the cabinet doors.

Ryan knew that yes, his mother did keep some money in there, in a little pot with a lid. 'No,' he said, suddenly, 'no, not in there. Stay there. I know where she keeps it.'

He rushed out of the room.

'Get us at least a twenty,' he heard Steve call after him as he raced up the stairs.

He went into his own room, opened the bottom drawer where he'd been saving money for that leather jacket he didn't really want. Forty-five pounds he'd managed to save. He picked it up, turned to go. As he turned, he caught sight of his white and sweating face in the wardrobe mirror. He halted. The face in the mirror, beneath the rearing rhino horn, showed palely a sympathy he seemed to see nowhere now – nowhere but here, in his own self-pitying image, always caught in a dusty mirror, bending and fawning before somebody else's will.

The Ryan reflected there – that pale, distorted anti-image of himself – who could recognise it? Who?

He looked down at the notes squeezed into his hand, looked back at the clown in the mirror. Quickly replacing twenty-five of the forty-five, the clown went palely padding back down the stairs.

Steve Bright looked at the twenty. 'This it?' he said.

'It was all I could find,' Ryan told him.

They stood staring for a moment, eye to eye. Ryan felt foolish and uncomfortable, intimidated by the suspicion in Steve's face.

But a new, refreshed round of rapping and thumping at the doors and windows caught Steve's attention. 'There they go,' he said. 'Now, you do your stuff.'

'What stuff?' Ryan asked.

'Out there. Give them something.'

'Something?'

'Yeah. Get out there.'

'What for?'

Steve glanced impatiently to one side. 'What is it with you? You gotta give them a bit of something. I'll sell them the rest. Well?'

Ryan shifted uncomfortable. 'Well – what?'

'Well get out there then. You're the Rhino Boy, aren't you? Aren't you?'

Ryan nodded, his rhino horn cutting the air.

'Well get out there and beast it up a bit. Go on. Go and do it for them. Get them going. Go on, animal. Go get 'em.'

Ryan stood there, palely blinking.

'Well what are you waiting for?' his father demanded of him. 'What you waiting for?'

Ryan shifted, swallowing, blinking.

'Well? Come on! What's the matter with you?'

'I–' Ryan said, trying to think, trying not to think.

'What? What's wrong with you?'

'I'm sorry. I can't.'

'Can't? What's can't? I'm not interested. Listen, I'm your old man, you'll do what I say.'

'Yes, but I–'

'Listen!' Ryan's old man shouted, his pointy, bristling face moist in Ryan's. 'I owe some people, right? You'll do as you're – you'll do it. Out there. Give them some pictures, I'll do the rest. You hear me, Rhino Boy? You hear me?'

Ryan, looking down, nodded.

His old man nodded back, passing by him, opening the front door.

Ryan could hear the click and clatter of long lens photo equipment being shortened, being prepared for close-up, for real close up.

'And make it good, animal,' Steve Bright said, as his son stepped out of the door into the flash-attack.

Tears were falling unseen and unheeded from Ryan's animal nose as he hoofed at the ground for his audience.

Flash guns were popping, all the other animals there baring their teeth, roaring with delight.

Ryan ran in as Steve stepped into the flashlit front garden, his hands held palms upward for silence.

'Ladies and Gentlemen of the press,' Ryan heard Steve Bright shouting, as he closed the front door behind him, as he crumpled onto the floor, falling where the morning red-topped newspaper usually fell.

He tried to put his tear-soaked face into his hands. The huge, hideous horn pressed against his fingers. He grabbed at it, trying to haul it from his head. His head was torn from side to side. The horn remained part of him, his skull, his brain, his whole way of thinking.

He slapped at it. The slap reverberated through his brain. He slapped again. And again. And again, but his hands turned to fists, his fists fought against himself – against the anti-image that was now Ryan Bright, that was everything except that which he now wished himself to be.

He sat staring at a blank TV screen. All the signs were that too much, far too much was happening.

The night clung to him like a cold friend. Only here, now, in the street lamplit half light, could Ryan feel anything like left alone. The lamplit street outside was deserted but for an old man walking his dog. All the other hounds had deserted after the photo session and his father's frantic tabloid negotiations.

Ryan curled up cold on the sofa, dreading the next day, and the day after that, and the day after that. Dreading every day, every day, for the rest of his life.

o o o

Tomorrow, a white stretch limo was coming to collect Ryan and take him to his hospital appointment. The rip-roaring *Red Top* newspaper was sending its VIP car and driver for him. They wanted to protect their forthcoming investment, they said. Which meant that Steve Bright was going to force Ryan to talk to their reporters for money.

Steve Bright had debts, he said. Some very nasty people he owed money to. He had to have it. He was sure, he said, that Ryan, his own son, would understand.

Ryan was not so sure his own, unknown father understood anything. He wasn't sure Steve was capable of that kind of understanding, even if Ryan had been capable of explaining it to him. Which he wasn't. So he didn't bother trying.

Which meant Ryan was going to have to suffer further humiliation in the morning tabloids, just to appease his father and pay off that man's gambling debts.

What else could he do?

Ryan couldn't see any way out of any of it.

Which meant the *Red Top* sending an over-conspicuous motor in the morning, publicly announcing every move Ryan had to make.

Ryan curled up in the cold night, alone on the settee. He hugged his knees, whispering to himself.

'I hate you,' he whispered, to the horn on his head.

'I hate you,' to that horn, and to the gutter press.

'I hate you,' to the horn, the gutter press, his father, and everything else.

'I hate you,' he whispered. To himself.

Two

Ryan and Dan

'Yes, but what's Dan have to come for? What does she have to come for?'

'I thought you might like to have both of us there, for support. Dan really wants to go with you.'

'Yeah, to have a ride in that car, that's the only reason,' Ryan said, sitting drained and dull at the table over the morning paper.

'Dan wants–'

'Dan wants a thump,' Ryan said, 'I know what Dan wants.'

'Give her a break, can't you?'

'Why can't someone give *me* a break then? It's a school day today. You can't just let– Danni's the one who loves school, not me.'

'Yes, don't I know it.'

Ryan looked dryly at his mum as she fussed in the kitchen. 'So why can't you just do what you normally do? Why do you have to–'

'Look, Danni doesn't want to go to school today, all right? I've decided to make today a holiday, all right? It's my decision, all right? So leave her alone for once. Just for once. All right?'

Ryan looked again at the morning papers. No, in actual fact he was not all right. Very far from all right, if you must know.

○ ○ ○

Dan was looking out of the window upstairs at the sightseers gathering round the longest white car you've ever seen in your life. The windscreens were smoked so that no one could see in. Ryan was going to like that much about it, if nothing else.

And the chances were, Ryan would like nothing else about it. Chances were, Ryan was going to hate everything, like he usually did. No, like he *always* did.

Dan never knew what to do for the best. It didn't seem to matter what happened, Ryan always seemed to find a reason to have a go.

There was still a bruise on Dan's forehead where Ryan had slammed her against the door. It was as if she was to blame for the thing growing out of Ryan's head.

It got so bad sometimes with Ryan that Danni often felt blamed for just about everything. Whatever went wrong, whatever, the blame always seemed to be aimed in her direction. Sooner or later, Ryan would try to give the blame to his little sister.

If it wasn't like that, then why would Ryan want to go and push Danni's head straight into the front door?

○ ○ ○

Ryan cringed to see the state of the car they'd sent round for him. He'd looked out to see what Dan was going on about now and there it was, by the kerb, but stretched over the length of about three front gardens.

All Ryan wanted was a big hat and a pair of dark glasses. But instead, he had to have this, this– spotlight on him.

Dan had to go on and on about it as if it was something good. Their mother, she went all flustered, her feathers puffed up, clucking and preening, preparing herself to be seen by the neighbours. As if she was proud. Proud to be seen like this, with her son like this.

Like this!

His animal visage on pages three and four and five. His beastly posturing with his sire of a father pictured, posted, proud behind him at the door.

She had panicked, his mother, flustered to find that Steve Bright had been there yesterday. She squawked, flapped flying to her little money pot in the sideboard cabinet, frantically ripping off the lid. 'Has he been in here? Has he been in here?' she squawked, scrabbling the notes out, rifling through them.

'You didn't give him any money, did you?' she said to Ryan.

Danni was there. 'Why? Why wouldn't you give him any money?'

'Just don't give him any,' she said to Ryan, as if he had asked the question. 'And don't go letting him in the house any more when I'm not here,' she said.

'Why not?' said Dan.

'Just don't,' she said, to Ryan again, as if Dan hadn't said anything at all.

So annoying, that woman.

So, so annoying.

○ ○ ○

It didn't matter what Danni did, it was always wrong, according to Ryan. Oh sure, she tried to make fun of him. Of course. He was her brother after all. That's what brothers are for, isn't it?

But Dan knew when to stop. Ryan was going through it enough, what with everyone at school taking it out of him. She tried to help him. But it never seemed to help. Ryan would want to push someone's face through no matter what Dan said, good or bad. There was no winning.

Look what happened when Dan even so much as offered a bit of information about what a rhino horn consisted of. What happened? Ryan got mad about it, what else?

Dan tried to make Ryan think he looked all right, or that it was cool that he was famous. Nothing did any good. So, might as well try and stay out of it. Which is what Dan had been trying to do when the *Daily Red Top* had said who their father was.

○ ○ ○

Ryan didn't like it. They were all going off to the hospital to see about having this thing removed from Ryan's face. Plastic surgery, they said he needed. Plastic surgery!

They had an appointment to see Mr Johnson, the plastic surgeon, that morning at eleven o'clock.

Ryan was going to end up with a plastic mask for a face. That was going to do a lot for his image. Who'd want to go out with a boy with a great plastic disk on his forehead like something out of some weird sci-fi serial on TV?

He supposed that'd be plastered all over the papers next. Robot Boy or something they'd be calling him next. Nylon Nut.

Ryan could already hear the annoying, really annoying laughter of his mates.

Mates?

Who had any mates left?

Was there anyone left who was not all out to make him feel ridiculed, intimidated, threatened?

No one.

Absolutely no one.

o o o

Dan couldn't do a thing right, could she. Just look at what happened this morning when Ryan was going on to their mum about ending up with a plastic face.

'What am I going to look like?' Ryan was going. 'What am I going to look like?'

'I don't know,' she said.

'I do,' he said. 'I'm going to look like a freak with a plastic head on, like that robot out of–'

'No,' Dan said to him, trying to help, 'no, it isn't like that. Plastic surgery doesn't actually use any plastic like that. They just–'

'Well why do they call them plastic surgeons then, div-head?'

'They don't.'

'Then why is everyone telling me I'm going to see a

plastic surgeon? What, is he made out of plastic or something?'

'No, that's just what they're commonly called–'

'Oh! Commonly called, is it? You little–'

'Now then! Now then!' their mother had to go, intervening, as she did, as she always did.

Danni knew their mum always had to intervene, as protection from another attack. That's what it was like. It didn't matter what was said. If Dan tried to make fun of him, Ryan would start to threaten. If Dan tried to help him, the same threats. There was no winning.

o o o

Even his own sister tried to make Ryan look like an idiot. That know-all had to know all there is to know about what plastic surgery's all about.

If it's all about skin grafts and things, why do they bother to call it plastic surgery?

And what's all this about taking some skin off of Ryan's backside and sticking it on his face? Nice. Hope they pick a clean bit. Nice.

Dan reckons to know everything, like someone special or something. The way their mother always wants to treat her, you'd think she was something special. She treated Dan so differently. Why did she have to do that?

o o o

Danni was confused. There was no understanding how things happened like this. How did it all get so troubled, with everyone being so horrible to each other?

96

Why did it have to be like this?

Look at Ryan now. Look how surly he was, how upset and ready to start.

Dan didn't really want to go with Ryan to the hospital and see about having his head sawn off. Unless they really were going to cut his head off, and sew on something a bit more reasonable.

Perhaps Ryan's brains went all the way to the end of that horn? Maybe when they hacked it off half his grey matter would come tumbling out like an erupting volcano? Not that it'd make too much difference, as far as Danni could see. Ryan didn't seem to us his brains too much anyway.

Dan was beginning to want to be at school. This morning didn't feel right for it, but it also didn't feel right for spending the day hanging round the wards and waiting rooms with a snarling, bellowing brother.

Still, there was always the limo. That was pretty neat. You couldn't really pass up a ride in a limo, could you? No matter what, you couldn't pass up a ride in a stretch limo.

∘ ∘ ∘

The truth was – Ryan didn't like to have to admit it – he didn't, couldn't like Steve. Steve didn't give him anything *to* like. He didn't give him anything, in fact.

But Ryan didn't want to have to think about it. There was too much to worry about today as it was.

'Are you ready, Ryan?' his mother kept going to him, on the way past.

'Are you ready?' she kept going, rushing from one ground-scratching position to the next.

Ryan had been ready for about four hours. Or he could have been ready four hours ago, if he'd wanted to be. That's how long he'd been awake.

Lately, he'd been sleeping whenever. During the afternoon, whenever. The night-time though, it, of all times, seemed to want him awake. Too awake, most nights, looking out of the window to be sure the press were all safely tucked up. He'd tuck them up all right, given half the chance.

Half the chance? Fat chance.

'Are you ready, Ryan?' she said, flapping by.

He watched her go. He listened as she called up the stairs for Dan.

'Are you ready, Love? Come on, Ryan's waiting to go.'

As if he'd said anything.

He didn't have to. Ryan never seemed to have to say anything any more. They all wanted to do his talking for him. Ryan's waiting. Was he?

Yes, he supposed he was, but he hadn't said so.

Ryan hadn't said a thing.

o o o

Dan couldn't pass up the chance of a ride in a car like that. You should have seen it. She couldn't believe it inside. So big. So big!

You could slide on your combat trousers from one side to the other. Polished leather seats. Really deep carpet.

All sorts of cabinets for drinks and things. Mostly empty, or locked. But still.

They'd got into the thing, the driver opening the door as Ryan approached and flung himself in head first. Horn first. In. Out of the way. He'd have covered his head with a blanket like they do on the news if their mother had allowed him. She told him not to be such an idiot. It was only the neighbours, she said.

He'd have done it though, Dan could tell.

In he went, like a gazelle, horn first as if he was going to fight it out with another antelope.

Dan came next, peering into the big dark cave of the car before stepping in.

Then they waited while their mother kind of strutted, yes, strutted down the garden path, paused to peer about at the neighbours' houses, before lowering her backside into the dark, black back seat. She lifted her legs, slowly bringing them into the car's dark comfort.

Dan was nearly laughing.

Ryan, Dan could see, was nearly crying, he was boiling so hot with frustration and embarrassment.

Dan decided to keep out of his way as much as possible. Which was quite possible in the back of that massive car. Like half a football pitch, it was.

The driver didn't have to say a word. He didn't ask them where they were going, or anything. He closed the door on them, they didn't have to see him again. They felt him climb into the front, didn't feel the engine starting up. The whole thing just glided, slid like an arrow through the air, up the road and round the corner and away.

Dan was into all the cabinets. In one, a telephone. Not a mobile, but a proper 'phone.

'Look at this,' Dan said.

'Yes, put it back,' their mother said, quickly. 'Put it away. Leave things alone. It's not your car you know.'

Dan laughed. You couldn't see the driver. You could see out, people couldn't see in.

They pulled up at the lights. Dan was making faces at all the people gawking at them.

'Stop that!' – Mum again.

'They can't see me,' Dan told her.

'No, but I can.'

Dan let the window down by pressing a button. It wound down quickly, smoothly, with this really great whirring sound. Dead smooth and rich.

'Wind that up!' – Mum.

As it went up, Dan was making faces at this man standing at a bus stop looking in at them.

'Bet he wishes he was in here,' Dan said, opening another one of those cabinets.

As this one opened, another whirring sound, and, you wouldn't believe it, a little TV on a tray came sliding out.

'Oh yeah!' Dan was going. 'Ryan, look at this. Only a TV set, isn't it? Look at that! Your own TV in your car. Ryan, look, it's got its own remote and everything. Is that cool, or what? Ryan, you've got to be a star to get a car like this, really, you have to be. You know, like what's-his-name off the–'

That's when Ryan went into one.

o o o

'Are you ready Ryan?' she kept on saying to him, even though he'd been sitting waiting for everyone else for about sixteen thousand hours.

Then calling up the stairs after Dan, saying, 'Ryan's waiting,' having only just asked Ryan if he was ready, and not waiting for an answer.

Ryan was screwing the newspaper in his fists, strangling the life out of the life-threatening images of himself. Ryan was there at the table wringing his own throat.

His mother was there, putting on her best coat and scarf as if this was some kind of royal outing for the king and queen of the housing estate.

Ryan dashed out of the door, rumbled down the garden path, head down, shoulders hunched. That great oaf of a padded driver, in a dumb grey suit and tiny peaked cap, saw him coming and stepped out. He looked like a bouncer in fancy dress, the oaf.

Ryan cringed, his head going down still further, shoulders coming further up. He fairly dived into that car, sliding himself across the ridiculously wide, leather back seat and into the corner.

He had to watch Dan clambering in next, all excited and wide-eyed like a fool.

Then another age while the royal pheasant came strolling down the garden path in her best, presenting herself before the neighbours, planting her backside on the seat before lifting her legs into the car.

I ask you! Ryan was cringing, bent double in the corner as the oaf of a driver clunked closed the door on them. Nobody had to tell him where to go. It was all arranged.

Ryan resented that. He had no choice, no say in the matter. He tried just to look out of the window, not to think about anything.

But Dan was in the car with him. Wouldn't you know it? Opening the windows all the time, looking in all the cabinets and at the stuff they had in them. It was all a load of old rubbish anyway, but Dan was into everything.

'Dan, wind that window up,' their mother was saying continuously. 'Leave that alone Dan . . . Dan, come out of there . . . Dan! Dan! Dan!'

Then the little ape goes and finds a television in a box. A little telly with a remote, nothing unusual. Except that Dan has to treat it as if it's the find of the century. It's as if they've never seen a TV set before in their lives.

'Look at this Ryan! Look Ryan! Cool! Ryan! Look, a TV set! Cool! A remote! Cool! Look Ryan! A remote! Cool! Cool! Cool!'

Ryan's teeth were being ground to dust.

'You've got to be a star,' Dan started going, telling Ryan that you had to be someone special to have all this rubbish. Telling Ryan! Telling Ryan!

Ryan couldn't stand it.

'Why don't you shut that idiot up!' he shouted at his mother. He found himself thumping the seats, kicking, lashing out. 'Just shut up! Just shut up!'

'Now then! Now then!' his mother was going.

Ryan was lashing out, wanting to smash everything, to

smash everything, to smash his way out of that car, out of that situation, out of every situation.

He was kicking, lashing out, thumping.

The car stopped, suddenly, with a little screech. A little screech of the tyres, a rocking of the suspension, the car had halted.

Ryan's mother looked at him. 'You've done it now,' she said. 'You've gone and done it now.'

∘ ∘ ∘

Danni could feel that huge, great, grey flannel driver lifting himself out of the front. The door next to Ryan opened, he was standing there, half-stooping, looking in at Ryan.

Dan was almost bursting with stifled laughter. Ryan was absolutely, absolutely witless, shrinking into the back of the seat under that big bloke's big-bloke stare.

'All right?' he said, after a while, the big fella. But only after a good long while.

Ryan just nodded.

Dan was very nearly wetting the back seat with all the swallowed laughter.

'Now maybe you'll calm down,' their mum said to Ryan as the car started smoothly off again.

'I will if you keep that idiot quiet,' Ryan said.

Meaning Dan. As if Ryan wasn't an idiot himself. *As if*.

'You leave Dan alone,' Ryan was told.

He did too.

Dan turned on the TV, flicked through the channels using the remote, found nothing, turned it off.

Ryan was dead quiet. They all were, but Ryan was red quiet, angry quiet, quietly seething, his teeth hard-wired together.

It didn't take long to get to the hospital. It wasn't that far away. Only a few stops on the train, so they were soon there, soon piling out of the car, with Ryan rushing off to prevent anyone getting a good look at him.

It didn't work though. Everyone got a good look at Ryan. Dan could see them all recognising Ryan the Noceros as they made a dash for the Out-Patients' department. So many people were stopping to gawp at Ryan, at his rhino horn, that Ryan was growing madder and madder. The more they looked, the redder Ryan became. He was boiling.

Dan could easily see it. Their mother could see it. They just couldn't catch up with him. Practically running, Ryan was, dashing through the crowd that had been completely silenced by his appearance.

Ryan went straight on through as if he knew where he was going. He didn't, of course, but trammelled on through as if he did.

He was trying to escape the faces, the curious pointed stares on all the out-patient faces, that was what he was doing.

His mum was after him, calling, 'Ryan! Ryan!' as if crying out to the crowd that this was, in person, the famous Rhino Boy.

He went flying through the out-patients, his head down, horn first, down a corridor and round a corner.

Dan was chasing after him: 'Ryan!'

Dan rounded the corner just in time to see someone there reach out and grab Ryan by the wrist. As he went to charge on past someone in a wheelchair, a hand stretched out and took hold of Ryan's wrist. Dan came breathlessly round the corner just as it happened. They all halted in the corridor.

The girl in the wheelchair seemed to have a pretty good hold of Ryan. It looked to Dan as if she was dragging Ryan down to say something to him.

Dan stopped to watch.

o o o

When they pulled up at the hospital, Ryan got himself away from that chauffeuring oaf as quickly as he could. But Ryan had forgotten how well-known he was. As he went for Out-Patients, the out-patients were there in their droves – *Red Top* readers with an eye for the recognition of a famous boy with definite rhinoceros tendencies.

Honestly, they all stopped in their tracks, people with ordinary, simple injuries that just bled and hurt in the normal, ordinary way. They stopped – bandaged, damaged and limping, half blinded and homeless, but all over interested in the horned apparition hurrying on through, flustered and red.

Red and flustered, Ryan the Horned Phenomenon raged on through, with his single parent singly calling out his name to the out-patient rabble.

Ryan raged through – thrashing, gnashing – his mother and Dan hot and cold on his heels. He didn't know where he was going. He passed through the foyer into a doorway, up a corridor and round a corner.

Ryan never noticed the girl in a wheelchair until her hand came out like lightning and gripped him round the wrist. He halted, trying to pull his arm free. But the girl had hold of him surprisingly tightly. She was pulling his arm down, pulling him down to look at her.

He had to bend down and take a look at her.

He looked at her head bent permanently down, her loose mouth hanging half-open. He saw the off colour of the teeth and the thick drool that hung from her lower lip and soaked into the white of her hospital top.

Ryan saw her eyes on him. Not fixed on his rhino appendage, but into his eyes. She was looking, this girl, straight into his eyes. Her young eyes were wrinkled, the skin around them wrinkled, faded.

Ryan flung her hand off his arm. Her head went flopping back, the line of drool breaking, falling.

Everyone wanted to grab at him, gaze at him. He wasn't having it. He dashed off up the corridor as his mother came flapping round the corner after him.

o o o

Dan watched Ryan fling the girl's arm away. Her head fell drastically back, remained there. Her hand still seemed to be holding out there in the air, still reaching after Ryan.

'You pig,' Dan whispered. 'You absolute pig.'

Their mother came flying by after Ryan, not pausing longer than to glance back at Dan. Dan watched her barge by the girl's wheelchair before disappearing round another corner.

Danni's head was shaking. That was it, the last and final straw. No one, but no one should be allowed to get away with that sort of behaviour. It didn't matter what he was going through, Ryan wasn't going to get away with it any more. He just wasn't. Dan was going to see to it.

She had had enough. She moved off down the corridor after her mother, and her brother.

○ ○ ○

Wherever he went, wherever he ran, they'd be there, staring at him, laughing at him, clutching at him. He couldn't take any more. There were limits to what anybody could persevere. Ryan's limits had all been reached. The all and sundry had driven him like a beast beyond that which could be endured.

He ran, crazed with fear and self-loathing, along the peopled runways, through a ward filled with hostile, spiteful women, out of a side door to a staircase. The stairs went nowhere but up. Ryan didn't, couldn't think about what he was doing. He climbed the stairs, breathlessly frantic, his beast breath snorting, steaming from his wide nostrils. The teeth in his snarling face were clenched hard, that face straining to get away. Just to get away. Like an animal from the wild caught desperate and lost in a sudden city, the rhinoceros plunged through another door, wildly, desperately lost. Another lost but overpopulated corridor stretched away before the beast. Everybody stopped and stared.

The rhino thrashed and stamped.

∘ ∘ ∘

Danni ran. She covered the ground much more quickly than her mum, who, in any case, had collapsed, breathless and gagging, waving Dan on up the corridor to go and find her brother.

He, she found, was easy to follow. Everyone noted when the wild animal, horned and dangerous, hooved by, grunting and grinding down the alleys between the wards. A few Danni quickly asked, Had they seen the *Red Top* superstar, but most simply pointed quite naturally onwards, knowing what she was after.

She ran up a staircase. It was the only place he could have gone. At the very top, through another door, Dan could tell he wasn't far in front. He had left a kind of startled disarray behind, a wake of curious surprise that had not yet begun to fade.

A crash, a scream, a man's voice in a sudden angered shout, reconfirmed to Dan that she was on the right track. She turned a corner. The corridor was a bedlam chaos of broken cups and spilt tea. A hot drinks trolley was over, everything spilt, a green-overalled woman standing pinned to the corridor wall, her hand over her mouth. Two men watched while another returned, shaking his head.

'He's mad,' she heard him say.

He's mad all right, Dan thought, as she picked her way through the broken cups and biscuits, sliding on a float of coffee in a slick across the floor.

She ran on to the end. But the end was not the end. It was the entrance to another staircase. This one went down. Only down.

Danni peered over the railing and down the stairwell. Several flights further down she could see a hand gripping and ungripping the banister rail, as the animal charged down and down. She could hear the dense snort of rhino breath heaving down, horned-head first, a force of brute instinct and wild fear.

'He's mad,' Dan whispered to herself.

'He *is* mad.'

o o o

The rhino ran up the stairs and out into another instantly silenced environment. The humankind stopped unkindly, stared. He could go back, but couldn't. Wherever he'd already been was too aware, too curious, too eager to catch hold of him. He could only charge on.

He charged, unthinking about where there was to go. There was nowhere to go. Nowhere, however, was a better place than the somewhere he had always been. Nowhere was a better, much better place. And worth fighting for.

So it was head down, horn up, blowing and bellowing down the alley-ways of people. He shoved them all aside, wheelchairs, beds on wheels, straight and crooked people alike. They blurred his eyesight into a red and white flurry, angry and afraid, red and white.

A man shouted almost into his face. He thrashed, casting the men and their metal machinery aside. A scream. A crash. Ryan thrashed. Water spilled splashing from the walls, cups and glasses smashing.

Ryan steamed, screamed through, a rhinoceros tipping aside a plains-jeep full of nasty riflemen and flash photographers. A man's nasty hands were quite suddenly on him, wanting to hold him back. The rhino thrashed free, its hard horn striking home into something fleshy and soft. Almost everything felt fleshier, softer than the horn. There was a grunt of pain, but not from horn-hard Ryan, running flat-footed across the flat plain with another great white hunter hard in pursuit.

He, the rhinoceros, plunged through another doorway and down the well of another staircase. His pursuer was left way behind as Ryan took the stairs down three at a time. His ivory-toed, numb feet looked separated from him, thundering under like the feet of another beast altogether.

Down he dashed, and down. The stairwell seemed to drip with moss and dank plantlife. The lighting changed, dimming as down he plunged, deeper and cold, into a strange semi-lit underworld of pipes and trays full of squirming black wires and little trapped lights in bowls along the wall.

The beast Ryan had lost its bearings. The red floors and dirty white walls told of a directionless purpose that was not Ryan's. Ryan's purpose was unknown here, lost, here in the dense basement as wet as cold tears. And alone.

Great brute tanks coated in fat white cladding displayed fearful dials. Somewhere a furnace clicked and lighted.

The Ryan-beast stared at the sound.

Then at another sound. Footsteps sounded loud on the stairs somewhere behind. The beast started, ran on in the wrong direction. Between the tanks he ran with no sense, with no direction but this wrong one, running into a tangle of pipes and dials and pumps and taps. He ran forward at the tangle in front, turned against the tanks on one side and on the other. He turned and turned, the whole dreadful twisted squirms of glass and metal, the sides of the tanks, bellying out in a claustrophobic cage with only one way out. The way he had just come.

The beast turned.

Footsteps approached its only exit.

The beast's back arched. The horned head went down. The eyes blazed, mad. Ready to charge, ready to barge its way, the only way, out.

o o o

Danni charged down the stairs after him. He was mad, she'd heard that man saying so. But she didn't need to hear him say so. She knew he was mad. He'd been driven to it, she knew, like an animal driven into a pen. That's where her brother was running to, she knew. She'd seen the fury of it in him as he'd spiralled down the stairs too far. This far down, the basement ducts and pipes swirled like brain matter round the walls and across the ceilings. This far down, as far down as it was possible for Ryan to go, the unseen madness way below the normal is seen, curly and wet, twitching and cringing, its nerves laid out for all who look to see.

Dan walked carefully between the subterranean grey matter of a seemingly sane world. Up above, far above, in the squeaky-soled corridors, medicine set about the job of nursing, caring for the many but explicable ailments. Here though, the insane whirl of pump and pipe held hard a captive furiousness that wanted only to bend and break and escape.

Dan saw him captured there in another cruel cage. He was out of his mind. Furious with fear and outraged with shame, his beastly head sank, prepared to charge. Dan prepared herself to be charged. She took up all the space she could. There was only one way out. Through her.

'You're going to have to hurt me,' she told the animal. 'You're going to have to go straight through me. I don't care.'

o o o

'I don't care,' he heard her say.

His head was down, neck and back tensed, legs ready to forge forward. He was all rhino, beast-hard force and rage.

But, 'I don't care,' he heard her say again. Her voice entered his twitching animal ears like a reminder of another life. Recollections of life before the transformation, before the metamorphosis, tugged at him, bringing him to his senses.

He bristled with indignation. He didn't want bringing to any senses other than those instincts to fight and to survive. Those other senses, the old ones, they did nothing for him but bring him down, tear him up into little, fragmented parts. No, too much pain lay back there. He tensed, wanting the will to charge.

But the voice dragged him back, saying, 'You don't know the difference, do you?'

∘ ∘ ∘

She saw, with the utmost terror, that he was about to charge her down. She was afraid of him, like never before. But she wasn't backing down, not like this.

He didn't know the difference between a hand held to his face in threat and one held out in friendship. That was the trouble. That was how he had come to this. Every friendly hand had fisted, threatening him, until he had lost the ability to discern the difference.

'You don't know the difference, do you?' Dan said to him. She could hear the fear in her own voice as she said it. But she said it, then said it again.

'You don't know the difference between an enemy and a friend, do you?' she said.

∘ ∘ ∘

'You don't know the difference,' he heard her say. He could hear the fear in her voice. She was afraid of him.

He halted, breathing, breathing. No, he did not know the difference, because there was no real difference between enemies and friends. All hands of friendship turned into fists, sooner or later. He had too much experience not to have recognised the truth. He could trust no one. No one.

'What do you want?' he said, glaring at his sister.

'I want you to choose not to hurt me,' she said to him.

He halted, his eyes closing. He had hurt so many people, so many people. But always because he had no choice.

Dan stood in the space between the huge white tanks, giving him his choices back. He felt the responsibility of choice flushing his animal insanity away, folding him down onto the filthy floor.

He sat back against the mess of pipes, breathing heavily, his eyes closed. Dan, he could hear, was moving closer towards him. He tried to hold his hands to his face, but the huge horn got in the way.

He opened his eyes. Dan stood looking down on him. 'What do you want?' he said.

'I want to know why you had to hit Anil Patel.'

'I don't know,' he said. 'I don't know. How should I know? Why don't you ask me about something I *do* know?' he asked her, looking up at her. 'Eh? Why don't you ask me about our father? Eh? Ask me, why don't you?'

He glared up at Dan. She, seemingly unaffected,

remained where she was, without a movement, other than just the slow slide of her eyes.

'I'll tell you about him then, shall I?' Ryan barked up at her. She blinked, slowly, nothing more. 'Well? Shall I? Or not?'

o o o

The truth was, it had always been easier not to know. Of course, Dan had heard rumours, stories of what her father was like and what he had done. Of course, she had sensed the damage done to her mother by this man. But leaving it all alone had always been so easy for her. Had always been made too easy for her.

Having to learn, at this stage, came hard. Not always painful, not hard in that way. But with a feeling of nothing. To feel pain and hurt the way her brother did about his father had always seemed preferable to this empty, nothing feeling, to feeling this dead, black hole inside. Ryan's rant and rage had always, in truth, seemed preferable to this.

'Go on then,' she said, at length, blinking down at him. 'Tell me.'

o o o

But Ryan only knew *his* father. Like he only knew his own hurt. He didn't know how Dan was affected by Steve Bright. To have told her, now, would be to tell her too much, much too much about himself.

He looked up at her as she stood blinking over him. He looked at her forehead, where she'd fallen from the stairs into the door. The bruised swelling had subsided, almost disappeared. No huge horn erupted, guiltily and painful, there. Dan just healed quite simply, easily regaining her old self, unaffected by everything that had gone before. She was too simple, too intelligent and self-assured, to be broken down by Ryan's tale of terror and neglect.

He shook his head. 'He's just a bloke,' he said. 'An ordinary bloke, in a pub every day, wasting his life like a million others. He drinks every day in the Bald Eagle in town. He goes from there to the betting shop. That's it. He's nothing. There's nothing more to tell.'

○ ○ ○

A silence whirred and gurgled through the pipes surrounding them. The silence was an absence of speech. Dan let it go by.

Her brother was right. The drinker in the Bald Eagle meant nothing. But that didn't mean that there was nothing more to say.

○ ○ ○

The watery silence gurgled by. Ryan waited. There was nothing more to say.

At least he thought so.

Until Dan asked him again why he hit Anil. He sighed. She asked him why, as if he had the choice.

'I hit him because Jim Wire told me to,' he told her. 'I hit him because I had to.'

He watched her shake her head.

'And on Saturday,' he told her, 'we'll be back. We'll be waiting for him and his sister outside the Mosque. And I'll be there. I have to be.'

∘ ∘ ∘

'No you don't,' she said. She watched him shake his head. 'You don't have to do anything.'

He shook his head.

Dan, slowly, held out a hand to him. He looked up at it there in front of him.

∘ ∘ ∘

Her hand was out in front of him, with her telling him he didn't have to do anything. *She* was telling *him*! What did she know? Just, what did she ever *know*?

He slapped the hand away.

∘ ∘ ∘

He slapped the hand away, shot up, shoved Danni aside. 'Where are you going?' she said.

∘ ∘ ∘

Where was there *to* go? There was no getting away, no escape, anywhere.

'Where do you think I'm going?' he said. 'I'm going wherever I'm told to go. What choice do I have, in any of it?'

∘ ∘ ∘

Dan, her slapped hand still held out, watched him slop

away between the heavy tanks. He trudged round the corner on his own and out of sight.

Dan shook her head. He still doesn't know the difference, she thought, between an open hand, and a fist.

Three

Dan and Ryan

Waiting, hidden outside the Mosque, not too sure exactly what time to expect Anil and his sister to appear. Waiting much longer than anticipated. Some of the excitement and fear of what was likely to happen had evaporated, leaving a kind of nervous boredom, restlessly and repeatedly yawning.

All of which re-reversed into a renewed, excited fear, as Anil appeared with his older sister in the entrance to the Mosque, and started up the road.

Danni Bright stopped yawning, gathered all cast-off fearful excitement, started up the same road after them. But at a distance, not wanting to be spotted, while having always to keep them clearly in sight. Dan had to be sure to be there when something happened.

When something happened, it would be good, or it would be bad. Someone had to try to ensure which.

o o o

Started off up the road more fearful than excited, more tired than confused. Ryan had spent the whole day yesterday, Friday, grappling with the realisation of what he was going to have to do.

Jim Wire was going to threaten Anil and his sister. Jim

Wire was going to expect Terry and Ryan to be there backing him.

Jim Wire, Ryan knew, was one day going to do something very, very stupid. And, most likely, very nasty. Ryan wanted, had to be sure he wasn't there behind Jim when it happened. Terry could, for all Ryan now cared. Terry was lost to him.

Terry was nothing but what Jim, or anyone like Jim, would make of him. But not so Ryan. Not now, anyway. Ryan had his own conscience back. It was this thing that kept him awake all night, kept his stomach churning, his head spinning. Ryan's conscience sprouted, horn-like, out of his head, rhino-haired and hard.

Ryan's hard-headed conscience would lead him up the road to keep the rendezvous as arranged. Only now, Ryan was going to have to follow his conscience up the street to deny Jim Wire, whatever the consequences. Whatever consequences he would have to suffer, he would do it. He would even fight with Jim, if it came to it.

Ryan had a rhino horn sprouting from the exact dead centre of his forehead. This, this hard-hatted conscience, was what he could attack Jim with, if necessary. He hoped, dizzily prayed that it would not be necessary. Jim Wire not only looked and acted tough, he *was* tough. Hard as wire, Jim, and very reckless.

Ryan swallowed his own rising stomach as he tried to think of the limits beyond which Jim Wire would not go. He breathed erratically, trying to avoid the idea of Jim's fists flying, his big grinding boots capped with metal.

No – Ryan would not think of the consequences. He

would do the act, the right thing for once in his life. Now, again, he had no choice. The consequences of not doing it right were even more horrific. He may not be physically hurt by giving in to the pressures from all the wrong ones, but he had to live with himself. Which was not easy at the best of times.

He had decided, after all the sleepless nights, that he couldn't face, any longer, being the Ryan Bright he had read about in the papers. He couldn't bear being him – him, only more so, the newspaper Rhino Boy made worse and wilder by the intensified bullying his so-called mates were set to do today.

This Ryan Bright, *this one*, not the journalised version, the reported upon, the public freakshow on show daily, but *this one*, he was going to put a stop to it all. Yes, all of it. That meant stopping Jimmy Wire, stopping Steve Bright, stopping the red-topped dailies.

This Ryan Bright even started to feel a little reckless himself, a little bit brave, as he stomped up the road in his boots and jeans, head down, soon-to-be-removed hair horn heaving a way through the heavy air.

A pair of girls he recognised from school were coming up the other way. Just as this Ryan Bright was feeling slightly brighter, the pretty and ugly pair went too silently by him, breaking into giggles and semi-stifled snorts of laughter just barely behind his back.

Ryan's head dropped still further. His cheeks, his whole face blazed with embarrassment and shame. But Ryan's rhino-dense conscience was out in the open now. He had dreamt last night of strange disfigurements – the horrifying thing was that they were not his own. Not his own, but of his making. As if he had harmed someone else, damaged them, so that their disfigurement, so that everybody's disfigurement had become his own. And his own shame.

Now, after everything that had happened, after last night and the night before, after the dreams that had gripped him, forcing him to relive his dive too deep down with Dan into near-madness, he was never going to hide his face away again. Never succumb to fear and to the idiot pressure of his peers, no matter how afraid he was.

○ ○ ○

The trick was to keep a careful distance while holding the pair quite definitely in sight.

Part of what had to be done, Dan hoped, had been done. But, to be sure . . .

Yesterday, Friday, had not been easy: taking the note from their mother excusing Dan for having taken a day off school, with the intention of adapting it and spreading it over two days, not just the one – Dan felt bad about that. Then pretending to go off to school at the normal time, knowing that the note wouldn't be handed in until Monday morning.

The bus to school came the same as ever yesterday morning, but as the bus sailed by the school gates, Danni Bright's face could still be seen looking out of the window. That same face remained in place until the bus pulled in at the terminus in the centre of town. That face, puffa jacket, bag, could have been seen exiting there, making its way up Terminus Street towards the shopping centre.

In fact that face would have revealed, had anybody looked, a distinct lack of confidence in knowing where it was going. It wandered through the streets looking for a sign.

The sign it was looking for it found, eventually, much later, hanging outside the Bald Eagle. The pub looked open. Dim yellow lights were on inside, showing a few shady figures moving through the gloom.

The face had looked up at the sign, at the windows, the dim inside lights, the few smoky people.

Then Dan lost her nerve.

o o o

Yesterday, Friday, Ryan had spent the day desperately anguished, huddled tense and aching over what he should do. The telephone had kept bleeping every ten minutes or so. Its insistence broke Ryan's thinking into segments – similar chunks. At the beginning of each Ryan would find himself starting over. How many times he went through it all, he couldn't tell. Hundreds. It felt like thousands. It felt like his whole life.

The telephone broke it down, startling him every time into another, after another fearful blank stare. The bleeps would continue like an alarm for a minute or so, then stop. Ryan's mind would creep back out, sifting through, sifting through.

In the end – the end coming thousands, lifetimes

worth of sifts-through later – Ryan deliberately snatched up the receiver.

'Hello.'

'Hello. This is the features desk at the *Daily Red Top* calling for Ryan Bright. Is he available to speak to at all?'

Ryan sat staring, his lips twitching.

'Hello?' the telephone voice went again. 'Are you still there? Hello?'

'I'm still here,' Ryan said at length.

'This is the features desk at the *Daily Red Top* calling for Ryan Bright,' the features desk's female voice said again, word-perfect. 'Is he available to speak to at all?'

Again Ryan sat gagging, swallowing his own words.

'Is Ryan Bright available to speak to?' the features woman wanted, more insistently, to know.

'Er, no,' Ryan said.

'No? He's not available?'

'No. He's not. Not available.'

'Can you tell me when he will be available, please?'

'Er . . . oh, yes. I can. Never.'

'Never?'

'No. Never. He's never going to be available to talk to you, or to anybody else. Never.'

'May I ask who I'm speaking to, please?'

'Yes, you're speaking to Ryan Bright. Ryan Noceros. *You're* speaking to him, right now, for the last time. I'm never going to speak to you–'

'I'm sorry, but we understood–'

'No! You didn't understand.'

'In conversations with your father–'

'And he didn't understand. Listen to me now. Don't call back. I will never, never speak to you, or to any of the other papers. Now goodbye, for ever.'

Ryan, his heart beating so fast and so loud that he could hear it pumping inside his own ears, replaced the receiver quite calmly. His face was paper-white.

Now he'd done it. Steve Bright was going to be mad. He was going to be violent-mad.

Now, Saturday early afternoon, he stomped up the road knowing that everyone was going to be that mad at him. He was on his way to face the danger that was Jim Wire. He was going to have to face the possibly greater threat of Steve Bright. But he was going to face it. All of it.

o o o

Yesterday, Friday early afternoon, while her brother was finding nerve enough to slam 'phones down on the press, Dan's had gone completely. Looking through the weeping, drab window of that brown pub, all bravado suddenly drained away. There was no going through with it. Out of the question, just to walk into a pub alone and start looking round for someone. There was no just going up to someone, someone recognised only from a meeting at a bus-stop and a picture in a newspaper, and saying, 'Now I know you're my father.'

Danni pictured Steve Bright laughing at the bar there, with lots of other men standing round smoking and drinking. All of them would laugh as Steve offered to buy Dan a drink, a pint of beer or something. A whisky or something. She heard them all laughing. There was no going in.

Another hour of that Friday afternoon was wasted, just gone, swinging a bag through the halls of the shopping centre. Dan seemed to be looking for something, something to say what should be done, or how to do it. The clothes and shoe shops told of nothing, sold Dan nothing, despite all their best efforts. Dan wasn't buying, looking merely, for good reason, for a little, tiny little bit more reason than her arrival on the bus had brought.

Settling for a cup of tea, Dan watched the people come and go. How they didn't bother watching back. How they peered and poked into the windows and doorways of the shops, the purpose evident on their moist, twitching faces. Dan felt fascinated by them, by the way in which they all seemed to be something similar to one another, with the observer held in fascination, in ever so slight disgust, on the outside.

Feeling like the rank outsider, Dan swung back to the beer- and tear-stained Bald Eagle. The delay had done nothing for her resolve. Her confidence just wasn't here in this big town, under this grim grey sky, in the street outside a soiled and sour public house.

Once more Dan looked in at the wet windows running in something like condensed nicotine. Looking up at the pub sign, the bitter fierceness in a bald eagle's disapproving stare, the eagle frowned down, directly, disturbingly.

As Dan stared up, the pub doors opened, three men came out and turned the corner.

One was immediately recognisable in his sawn-off T-shirt, the bullet-belt and boots. The other two were wearing dark suits and ties under their heavy black overcoats. The other two were big. Very big.

One of the big two halted, turned to face Steve Bright. The other stood behind him. The first one shoved Steve back against the pub wall. He looked past them, but not at Dan.

Steve Bright looked past the two huge overcoats at nothing. His face was one of absolute terror.

Dan could see the terror on Steve's face as the first of the two spoke to him. Dan watched the man speaking, his face so close, so very close to Steve's.

The other man, the second overcoat, had moved round so that they both had Steve pinned against the wall. One of them moved suddenly, bracing himself as if to do something terrible. The look on Steve's face told Dan that this man, that these men were about to do something terrible to him.

Stepping into the road, Dan called, 'Dad! Dad, I'm here. Dad!'

Walking towards the three of them, Dan was calling louder and louder. One of the overcoats looked round.

Steve Bright looked at Dan's face as that face called, 'Dad! Here I am. Dad!'

Dan walked right up to them. The overcoats turned, saying nothing. Dan walked between the dark fabric curtains of their clothing.

'I told you I'd be here, Dad,' Dan said, taking Steve Bright's hand, taking him off the wall, walking him through the dark fabric curtains and away. 'You said you wanted to take me shopping for my new trainers,'

Dan was saying as they walked hand in hand up the road towards the shopping centre.

'I've been looking for you everywhere,' Dan said to him as they went.

Looking up, Dan saw that Steve Bright was weeping, his whole face wet with tears.

o o o

Now, Saturday early afternoon, Ryan lost his nerve.

On his way to meet Jim Wire for the showdown, all his good intentions departed suddenly under the growing reality of what he was going to do. He felt sick. His mouth had dried up. He tried not to think about it, to concentrate on simply keeping his legs going. He took one step after another.

But every step ate through the time and distance between himself now and himself then, when he was going to have to brave it out.

At one point he stopped. The air wouldn't enter his lungs properly. He stood in the street gagging.

'Come on,' he told himself. 'Come on now. Get on with it. Just get on with it.'

A man went by, staring at him, the rhino-horned phenomenon, standing on his own talking to himself. The man looked at Ryan as if he was a nutter. Ryan knew that in a way, he was. He must be mad to be going to do what he was. You had to be mad. Mad to do it, driven mad if he didn't. Either way . . .

Just keep walking, he told himself. Just walk. Just walk. Just walk.

So, he walked. He went there, to the place they said they would meet, at roughly the time they'd arranged. Here, just round this corner, they would wait in hiding for Anil Patel and his sister.

Ryan neared the spot.

As he approached the corner, Terry appeared. Ryan's heart sank. His sickness returned, the dryness in his mouth. The hands in his pockets sweated as wet as his mouth should have been.

Ryan stopped, waiting for Jim Wire to appear round the corner. He didn't. Terry came towards him.

Ryan tried to steady himself.

'Where's Jim?' he asked Terry.

'Haven't you heard?' Terry said.

o o o

Yesterday, Friday afternoon, Dan had decided to make happen what happened to Jim Wire. Steve Bright, tears of fear and relief wetting his face, had led Dan to the bus terminal. There they sat, in an uninhabited waiting room, draughty and cold, but quiet and isolated.

Dan watched Steve's face fall into his open hands. A weird silence hovered while Steve's shoulders shuddered as he fought to compose himself.

It all took some time. But eventually Steve's face came back out. Sniffing loudly, he looked at Dan.

Dan looked back at him. 'I know you know who I am,' she said.

Steve nodded. 'Course I do. But what are you . . . what were you doing there, in the street like that?'

'I came to see you.'

'You came . . . to see me?'

Dan nodded.

'I . . . you know. Lucky you were there,' he said, his moustached face breaking up again. 'I can't tell you what they . . . those blokes . . .'

'Who are they?'

Steve shook his head. 'I owe them money. Lots of money. I don't know how . . .' he said, his face breaking, head shaking.

Dan watched him.

'I can't tell you what they're gonna . . . what they're gonna do to me. I can't pay them. I can't . . .' His tears were falling again.

'I've got to get away,' he said. 'Right away, where they can't get me.'

'Where will you go?'

'I don't . . . listen. Why did you come to see me? How did you know where I'd be?'

'Ryan told me.'

'Why did you come?'

'To tell you some . . . some stuff.'

'Stuff?'

'About Ryan.'

'Oh. Ryan. What a thing he's got growing out of his head, eh?'

'That's what I wanted to talk to you about,' Dan said.

Steve Bright looked long and hard into his daughter's face. 'Haven't you got anything to say to me about yourself? I mean, I haven't exactly been there for you, have I?'

'No,' said Dan. 'But I don't know any different. Ryan does though.'

'Does he?'

'Yeah. He does. He remembers what it was like when you were there. He remembers it as something good.'

'He does?' Steve Bright said, genuinely surprised.

'Yes. He used to think you were really something. You know, really something.'

Steve Bright smiled, slightly, uncertainly. 'Did he?'

'Yes. That was before you turned up and humiliated him in all the papers,' Dan said.

Steve Bright said nothing.

'You understand what I'm saying?' said Dan. 'You humiliated him. Your own son. For money.'

Steve's head went back into his hands. Dan waited for him again.

'I'll go away. Right away. He won't have to see me ever again.'

'You don't need to do that.'

'Oh yes I do. I've got to go away. That mob, those gangsters, you don't know what they're likely to do to me.'

'Where will you go?' asked Dan.

Steve Bright didn't need to think about it. He sighed, said, 'I haven't got any money. But I can get away. I know how I can get away, safe, under lock and key.'

Dan looked and looked into Steve's face. The strange thing was, Dan thought, Steve and Ryan didn't look anything like each other. She, it had to be admitted, looked like Steve. A whole lot like him.

'Before you go,' Dan said, 'there's another thing.'

Steve Bright nodded.

'You know Ryan's mate, don't you?'

'Do I?'

'Yeah. Jimmy. Jim Wire. You know him, I know you do.'

'So?' said Steve.

'So,' said Dan, 'you're going to have to do something about him. Before you go, you're going to have to do something about Jim Wire.'

o o o

'No,' said Ryan. 'Heard what?'

'It's Jim,' Terry said, his face full of bitter regret,' he's been arrested.'

'Arrested?' Ryan said, almost giddy with relief. 'What, actually arrested by the police?'

'Yeah. Last night. And that's not all. Guess what else? You'll never guess. He was with your old man.'

'What!'

'Yeah. They did a garage. Last night. The two of them.'

'What? They what?'

'They tried to rob a garage. They got caught.'

'What, Steve Bright and Jim?'

'Yeah. Listen, it doesn't matter. We've still got to do what Jim said. Listen, right, we've still got to do it, right? Nothing's changed.'

'Oh yes it has,' said Ryan. 'Oh yes it has.'

Terry waited, unsure of what to do next. He didn't have anybody else to tell him what to do, so he waited.

'Everything's changed,' Ryan told him. 'It already had, but it's better now.'

'How do you mean?' Terry asked him.

But Ryan didn't answer. Terry waited, unsure of what to do. Terry was always unsure, always waiting to be told, to be guided or misguided. Guided or misguided, Terry really couldn't have told you what the difference was. He waited.

But Ryan was looking away, looking down the street.

Terry followed Ryan's line of vision to where Anil Patel and his sister had turned the corner, were slowing their pace towards them.

Terry turned to face them, glancing at Ryan for a clue as to the stance he should be adopting.

Ryan showed nothing.

Anil and his sister slowed their pace, stopped a few yards short of where Ryan and Terry stood facing them on the pavement.

Anil and his sister looked nervously at the two of them. Nobody spoke. They all stood there wondering what was going to happen next.

'What do you want here?' Anil's sister said at length.

Nobody spoke. Nobody moved.

'What do you want with us now?' Anil's sister said, her face full of hatred.

o o o

Dan, still pondering over Steve Bright's wetted face, his promise to do something about the situation between Ryan and Jim Wire, turned the corner after Anil Patel and his sister.

Turned the corner, Dan, to find Anil and his sister confronted by Ryan and Terry. Nobody spoke. Nobody moved. Dan waited.

'What do you want with us now?' Anil's sister said.

Dan couldn't see her face, but could hear the hatred in her voice.

Nobody spoke. Nobody said anything.

Dan looked at Ryan. It was obvious that he had noticed Dan there behind Anil. Taking a step forward, Dan said, 'They've come to apologise, haven't you Ryan?'

Anil and his sister looked round.

o o o

Ryan watched Anil and his sister look round at Dan, who had somehow appeared on the corner behind them. He watched as Anil and his sister looked back. He glanced at the ruby, red in Anil's sister's forehead, in a similar position to Ryan's rhino horn. For that moment, Ryan couldn't help but notice just how good looking Anil's sister was.

He could see Terry out of the corner of his eye. Terry was glancing at him, not knowing what to do.

'We want to apologise,' Ryan said, 'for what we did. For what I did especially. I'm sorry. So is Terry, aren't you, Tel?'

Terry looked at Ryan again. 'Yeah,' he said, unsteadily. 'Yeah. Sorry, like.'

Again they all stood there, nobody quite knowing what to say next.

'It won't make any difference,' Anil's sister said, 'you'll still have to go to court. You're still in trouble.'

'I know,' Ryan said, 'I *should* go to court. I did it.'

He walked forward, stepping up to Anil Patel. Anil's sister put her arm round her brother.

Ryan stepped up to him. 'Sorry Anil,' he said. 'I'm really sorry.'

Ryan found that he had tears in his eyes. He was remembering Anil's face, how it had spoken to him, asking, begging Ryan not to hit him, just before he'd hit him.

Anil was looking up at Ryan.

Ryan could see Anil looking at the rude eruption of the rhino horn sticking out of his forehead. Ryan stood his ground, allowing Anil to look, allowing Anil to see. Ryan allowed Anil to see the evidence of his guilt, the evidence of his new conscience. Ryan stood in front of Anil, not like a freak, but like a fellow victim.

They looked at each other, looked at each other.

Then Anil extended his hand, offering it to Ryan.

Ryan looked at the hand offered to him. He reached out and took it. He reached out and held the hand that was offered to him.

Four

Their Mother!

They could hear men's voices as soon as they came in. Dan and Ryan came into the house together, through the back door, into the kitchen. As soon as they came in, they heard the men's voices from the living-room.

They had been walking back together after meeting Anil and his sister. Terry had been with them part of the way.

Ryan had thought of asking Dan what *she'd* been doing there, but then thought better of it. He was glad she was there, that was all there was to it.

Besides, Terry was there as well, confused and unconvinced that they had done the right thing.

'What was *that* all about?' he was asking Ryan, as soon as they got far enough away from Anil.

'What do you mean, Tel?' Ryan said. 'I'd have thought even you could tell what that was all about. We just apologised to Anil. I did, and you did. That's what that was all about.'

'Yeah, bottled it more like,' Terry said.

Ryan exchanged a glance with Dan.

'You don't know,' Ryan said to Terry, 'what it takes, do you?'

'What you talking about?'

'You don't know what it takes,' Ryan told him, 'to tell

141

your so-called mates, to tell them you're not doing it any more.'

'What are you talking about, Rhino Boy?'

Ryan stopped. Danni, beside him, stepped slightly to one side.

Terry also stopped, the look on his face nothing but a response to the look on Ryan's.

Dan could see in Terry's nervous swallow his thinking again, and again, about what he had just said.

Ryan's head lowered, his face convinced, brute ivory and beautiful. 'What did you call me?' he said.

Terry said nothing. Dan could actually see the blood draining from his face.

'I came here,' Ryan said, slowly, deliberately, 'to have a fight with someone. Do you know who, Terry? I'll tell you. I came to have a fight to anyone who insults me or tries to . . . tries to . . .'

'Humiliate you,' said Dan.

'Humiliate me,' Ryan said, still staring into Terry's face. 'Anyone who tries to humiliate me, do you know what I mean, Terry?'

Terry nodded.

'And Anil never tried to humiliate me, Terry, never. Do you know what I mean?'

Terry nodded.

'Then I suggest,' Ryan said, 'that you get yourself out of my sight, before I really turn rhino on you. Know what I mean, Terry?'

'Yeah,' Terry said. Then, 'No . . . I . . . look, I . . . Ryan. I didn't think.'

142

'I know you didn't. You hardly ever do. Neither did I, before this happened to me,' Ryan said, touching his rhino horn. 'But it's all different now. Now I think about everything. And that's what you should do, Terry. Then you'd be able to make up your own mind for a change. Know what I mean, Terry?'

Terry, because he finally knew what Ryan meant, went. Ryan and Dan watched him go. They watched him look back, once, before he disappeared round the corner.

'He'll be all right,' Dan said.

'I don't really care if he isn't,' Ryan told her.

Dan didn't think that this was true, but she didn't say anything. Neither of them said anything more. They walked home together.

Ryan didn't fully understand what had happened. He needed to find somewhere quiet to sit and think it through. Dan didn't know what to say to him. She didn't know how much she should tell him about what she had done.

They walked home in silence. Coming in through the kitchen door, they could hear the men's voices in the other room. They glanced at each other before going in.

'Here he is now,' Ryan's mother said as he appeared in the living-room doorway.

Ryan looked at the two men sitting there, one on the settee, one in an armchair with a camera strap resting limply on his shoulder.

'These people are from the paper,' Ryan's mother said to him.

'I know,' Ryan said as Dan came in and sat at the dining-table. Ryan remained standing.

'We're from the *Daily Red Top*,' the one without the camera said.

'I know who you are,' Ryan said. 'What do you want?'

The reporter looked at Ryan's mum. 'They say you've told them you're not going to speak to them,' she said.

Ryan said nothing.

'Ryan? Is it true? Is that what you said to them?'

Ryan looked towards Danni, as if she could possibly answer this one for him. She couldn't, so didn't.

'Ryan?' his mother said.

The two press men were waiting to pounce, pens and paper and flash-cameras all poised and ready for action.

'Yes,' Ryan said, quite simply. He was looking at his mum, she at him.

But she was looking at him, right at or into him, in the way she usually only looked at Danni. She seemed to be speaking to him in some way. He, he found, was able to speak back.

Enough said, Ryan's mother seemed to be able to say. Enough said.

More than enough, Ryan seemed to say back.

'That's it then,' she said, out loud, turning to look at the reporter.

'That's it?' he said back. 'What's it?'

'He said he isn't going to talk to you.'

'But . . . but aren't you even going to ask him why?'

'No,' Ryan's mum said.

The reporter looked at Ryan, at his photographer, then back at Ryan's mum. 'But that's not enough,' he said.

'It is for me,' she said.

He looked at his photographer, who shrugged, seemingly unaffected. The reporter, however, was not so casual. His face, his gills, were reddening, beginning to glow. 'But I think you at least owe us an explanation,' he said to Ryan now.

Ryan did nothing.

'He owes you nothing,' Ryan's mum said. 'He owes nobody anything, least of all you.'

'But a contract's been signed!'

'Who by?'

'And there's the limousine. Somebody's got to pay for the limousine you all enjoyed using.'

'Then send the bill,' Ryan's mum said, 'to the person who signed the contract. Care of Her Majesty's Prisons, I'm sure it'll find its way to him.'

The reporter looked at his photographer again, who shrugged again. 'I suppose that's it then,' the photographer said.

'No, it isn't,' the reporter said. 'You're going to regret this,' he said to Ryan's mum. 'I promise you, you'll regret this. You broke his camera the other morning, you'll pay, I promise you.'

But the photographer stepped forward in front of the reporter. 'And I promise you, Madam,' he said, his mouth surrounded by a frizzy beard, 'that you will have to do nothing of the kind.'

'Now,' he said, turning to the reporter, 'I think it's time we left these people in peace, don't you?'

With a little, frizzy bow, he led the glowing, red-topped reporter out of the door.

Ryan's mother closed the door behind them. She came and sat at the table with Dan. Ryan joined them. For a minute or so, nobody said anything.

Ryan broke the silence, saying, 'Thanks Mum. You were really great.'

'Really great,' said Dan.

'Yes,' their mother said, 'but what I really want to know is, who made this dirty great ring on my table? Someone's burnt it with a cup of tea. That's what I really want to know. And – another thing – someone's gone and broken the bathroom cabinet. It looks like an elephant's charged into it. Who's going to pay for that? That's what I want to know. I'm fed up with going out to work every day,' she was going, going on and on and on.

Ryan looked at Dan. Dan looked up at the ceiling. Ryan smiled.

'You may well smile,' his mother started harping on at him, 'but somebody's got to pay, and it's not going to be me.'

'It'll have to be me then,' Ryan said, nearly laughing.

'You'd better get yourself a Saturday job then,' she told him. 'Someone's bound to need somewhere to hang their hat.'

Ryan looked at Dan. Their mother had cracked a joke. A joke! Their mother!

They looked at each other, burst into laughter. It was the first time Ryan had laughed at the rhino horn on his head. He laughed at the rhino horn, and at everything. He looked at Dan again. She, still laughing, looked at him. She was looking, Ryan could tell, not at the horn on his head, but at her brother.

He settled back to listen to his mum chirruping on about Saturday jobs. He smiled at his sister. She at him.

Ryan felt very, very glad to be home.

The Terrible Quin

Suddenly he moves. He grabs James . . . swings him round, throwing him over the edge . . .

'No!' Maria has screamed before she can even realise what has happened, or even that she has screamed.

Maria and James's father vanishes, without explanation. They want him back. They're desperate. But their search for him turns into a living nightmare. It's oppressive, relentless and nothing can prepare them for facing the Terrible Quin.

A gripping thriller guaranteed to have you on the edge of your seat.

Turning to Stone

Some things die, other things live. It's what happens.

'Please help me', she's saying to him. 'Tom, please, help me. Please, please help me.'

She hasn't slept. Anybody could see. She's been up, eating, being sick, making herself sick, eating again. Being sick again.

Now here she is, half killed by herself, by the madness that's got into her somehow.

This is the story of Tom, his big sister, Jazz, and someone else, who lives alone in a world of her own making. But she is the only person who can instil in them both the will to survive. It's about the weak and the strong, perception and reality. Powerfully told, compulsive reading – this is one book that you won't put down until you've read it cover to cover. Try it and see.